RUTHLESS MEN

Provost Captain Slade Moran hunts down Private Daniel Green, a deserter from the 2nd Cavalry accused of murder. But, when arrested, Green swears he's innocent. Upon returning to the fort with his prisoner, Moran is informed that trouble has flared up in nearby Lodgepole, where a saloon gambler has been caught cheating and soldiers want revenge. Three men have already roughed up the cardsharp, and now the saloon has caught fire. All suspicion points towards the soldiers of Fort Collins . . .

CORBA SUNMAN

◆

RUTHLESS MEN

Complete and Unabridged

LINFORD
Leicester

First published in Great Britain in 2014 by
Robert Hale Limited
London

First Linford Edition
published 2017
by arrangement with
Robert Hale
an imprint of The Crowood Press
Wiltshire

A catalogue record for this book is available
from the British Library.

ISBN 978–1–4448–3416–1

Published by
F. A. Thorpe (Publishing)
Anstey, Leicestershire

Set by Words & Graphics Ltd.
Anstey, Leicestershire
Printed and bound in Great Britain by
T. J. International Ltd., Padstow, Cornwall

This book is printed on acid-free paper

1

It was his animal-like reaction to danger that saved Slade Moran's life as he entered the derelict tumbledown shack. Thunder was growling in the darkened vault of the illimitable sky over the Colorado peaks miles to the south of Denver, and rain began to sluice down in torrents as he sought shelter. He was on the trail of a deserter from the 2nd Cavalry who had killed Tom Rogers, the sutler at Fort Collins, when he was caught stealing two bottles of whiskey. Moran, trying to avoid a soaking in the storm, had put his horse in a lean-to close by and hurried into the shack — straight into trouble. A lightning flash illuminated the dark interior of the dilapidated building and briefly highlighted a man's figure confronting him, one hand upraised, holding a long blade that glinted as it descended

1

quickly, aimed at Moran's chest.

Moran sidestepped, lifted his left arm to block the blow, and his forearm took the shock of halting the vicious movement. His right hand slid under his assailant's knife arm and seized the wrist from behind, his strength and forward movement forcing the descending blade away from his body. His left hand reinforced his right and he twisted the hand until the weapon fell from the man's grasp and clattered on the floor.

The man swung his left fist. Moran pulled his head down into his shoulders and tucked in his chin. Hard knuckles slammed against his right eyebrow. He countered by thrusting up his right knee and driving it into his assailant's groin. The man grunted and went down. Moran released his right hand from the man's wrist and drew his holstered gun. He struck for the other's head with the barrel of the weapon, felt the jarring impact at contact, and straightened as the man relaxed with a groan.

There was enough light in the shack to show Moran that his attacker was unconscious. He searched the man, relieved him of a pistol holstered on the right hip, and then used a short length of cord to bind his prisoner's hands behind his back before picking up the discarded knife. He relaxed to await the man's return to consciousness. A scar on the man's face showed up plainly in the gloom; it was all Moran needed to identify his attacker as Buster Green, the killer from Fort Collins. He had been trailing Green for a week since picking up his trail, and had, for the past two days, been expecting his quarry to turn at bay and fight for his freedom.

Green recovered from the effects of the blow and struggled to free himself. Moran watched silently. When lightning flashed again they gazed at each other.

'Who in hell are you?' Green demanded. 'I don't know you.'

'So why attack me?' Moran asked. 'You were prepared to kill a stranger?'

3

'I reckoned you was from Fort Collins. I ain't going back there. They'll hang me for sure.'

'You killed the sutler.' Moran held up the knife. 'Is this what you used?'

'How'd you know about that? Are you a soldier?'

'I'm Provost Captain Slade Moran of the Department of the Missouri. My job, among other things, is to pick up deserters and take them back to their units to answer criminal charges and stand trial.'

The lightning flashed again, searing through the shadows in a blaze of stark white brilliance. Green, gazing at Moran, saw a tall figure standing several inches over six feet, powerfully built, with a strong face, deep-set eyes, and a black moustache arched over a taut mouth. The lightning faded in seconds, but Green retained an image of the figure, and shivered. He had heard of Moran, and the stories told of the police captain's exploits sent a chill of fear through his cunning mind. He

renewed his struggle to get free, filled with sudden desperation, aware that if he was returned to Fort Collins he would hang for murder.

'What's your name?' Moran rasped, holstering his pistol.

'You know who I am,' Green responded.

'I do. But I need you to tell me.'

'I'm Private Daniel Green of the 2nd cavalry, stationed at Fort Collins.'

'And you deserted after killing Tom Rogers, the post trader at Fort Collins. I have a full description of you, Green, and the scar on your face is a clincher to your identity.'

'So I'm Buster Green. But I didn't kill Rogers. He was alive when I left him.'

'Save that for when we get to the fort. I'm not your judge. My job is to take you back in one piece, and there are two ways we can do that — the easy way or the hard way. It's up to you how. I've never lost a prisoner since I took this job, but I've toted in a number of

5

dead men because they chose the hard way. Do I make myself clear?'

'I get the message,' said Green harshly.

'So where's your horse?'

'It's along the trail. I sensed I was being followed so I hid it good.'

'We'll stay here until the rain eases,' Moran decided. 'If you know what's good for you then you won't give me any trouble.'

Green did not reply. He knew it would take them at least a week to get to Fort Collins, and a lot could happen in that time.

Six days passed, and Moran got to know Green fairly well as they travelled north back to Fort Collins. After a few days they chatted as if they were friends, but Moran never relaxed his vigilance and Green was always ready and waiting for the slightest chance to escape. But eventually Moran led his prisoner over a ridge and Fort Collins showed in the distance. Green was battered and bruised. Twice on the long

ride he had attempted to escape but Moran had earned his reputation the hard way, and Green could not see out of his left eye, which was considerably swollen and closed to a mere slit.

Moran eased himself in his saddle. They were covered in dust. Green was slumped in his McClellan; Moran rode stiff-backed and unbending. There had been no talk of the charges facing Green during the long hours of weary travel, and sight of the drab collection of barracks, offices, accommodation and stables animated Moran. There was no stockade around the fort, for the days of Indian attacks were over.

'It's the end of the trip, Green,' Moran observed. 'I think it's about time you came clean and told me the truth about the murder. There are several witnesses who swear that you threatened to kill Rogers, and finally carried out the threat.'

'And they're some of my so-called friends, huh?' Green laughed harshly. 'Who needs enemies with friends like

them? Talk's cheap, you know, and I was not the only trooper to call out Rogers. He was a cheap crook, and deserved what he got, but it wasn't me that killed him. Sure, I was in the trading post that evening, but I left to ride into Lodgepole, and when I sneaked back into the fort later Rogers was dead.'

'Can you prove that?' Moran demanded.

'I could, but it would be embarrassing for some people if I asked the lady in question to come forward and back my story.'

'What's a little embarrassment when your life is at stake?'

'I'll hang fire for a few days to see which way the wind is blowing,' Green said.

'It'll be easier all round if you either admit your guilt, or, if you're not guilty, give me facts to prove your innocence.'

'I'll do it my way,' Green said obstinately. 'You'd be better employed sorting out the problems at the fort.

The place is rotten behind its respectable face. There are more thieves and scoundrels here than there are fleas on a dog.'

Moran shook his head as he led his prisoner across the dusty parade ground and dismounted stiffly in front of the porch of the main building. A sentry armed with a rifle challenged him, and although he gave his attention to Moran, he could not keep his eyes off Green.

'I'm Captain Moran, provost department,' Moran reported. 'I can see you recognize my prisoner.'

'Yes, sir, it's Buster Green,' replied the sentry. 'I'll call the guard sergeant.'

He saluted and entered a nearby office, to return a few moments later with a sergeant, who saluted.

'I'm Sergeant Buller, Captain,' he reported. 'I'll put Green in the guardhouse, sir, while you report to Lieutenant Wiley, the officer of the day. He's in the company office — the next door along the porch to the left, sir.'

'Thank you, Sergeant.' Moran stepped on to the porch and paused to watch the sergeant take charge of Green, who was dragged out of his saddle and escorted off to the right by the sergeant and the sentry.

Moran entered the troop office. A big, fleshy soldier, wearing top sergeant's stripes, was seated at a desk just inside the door, and a lieutenant sat behind another desk situated beside an inner door that bore the legend COLONEL DENTON.

'Can I help you, mister?' demanded the top sergeant harshly.

'I'm Provost Captain Moran. I've just handed a prisoner, Private Green, Second Cavalry, over to Sergeant Fuller, to be lodged in the guardhouse.'

'Yes, sir.' The top sergeant sprang to his feet and saluted. 'I'm Top Sergeant Grimmer, sir. We had a message three days ago informing us that you were handling the investigation into Green's desertion and the murder of the post sutler. So you caught up with Green.

Did he give you any trouble, sir?'

'Nothing I couldn't handle,' Moran replied. 'When I arrested Green he stated that he did not kill Rogers.'

'I wouldn't expect him to admit to the charge, sir.' Grimmer shook his head and a faint smile flitted across his heavy, rugged features.

'I'm Lieutenant Robert Wiley, Captain.' The lieutenant arose from his desk, tall, slim, fair-haired, in his middle twenties. He came forward and shook hands with Moran. 'I'm Green's troop commander. We've investigated the murder, and there is a witness who states that Green told him he had killed Rogers. You'll need to talk to everyone on the post who knows something about the incident. Top Sergeant Grimmer has a summary of the evidence gathered at the inquiry, and we'll do all we can to assist you.'

'Thank you, Lieutenant. I shall be around for as long as it takes to check out the murder.'

11

'Colonel Denton will want to see you as soon as possible,' Wiley continued. 'There's been more trouble here at the fort since the murder. Headquarters have been informed, and they made a reference to you. Fresh orders for you have been forwarded from your department, pending your arrival.'

'Has my trunk arrived?' Moran asked. 'I need to get into uniform now.'

'It turned up a few days ago, and is in the quarters that have been assigned to you, Captain,' Top Sergeant Grimmer said. 'I'll conduct you to the officers' section when you're ready, sir.'

'I'll inform Colonel Denton of your arrival, Captain, and let you know when you can see him,' Wiley added.

Moran nodded and followed Grimmer out of the office. A squad of men were drilling on the square. The sentry was back guarding the headquarters area. Moran looked around critically, and decided that the post was being run efficiently.

'So what other trouble has cropped up, Top Sergeant?' Moran asked as they walked towards a row of wooden buildings on the far side of the parade ground.

'There's hostility between our soldiers and some of the people in Lodgepole, Captain. We've put the town off limits temporarily, but three men sneaked into town two nights ago and raised hell. The trouble started when word got out that the gambling set-up in Brannigan's saloon is crooked. There's a Fancy Dan gambler by the name of Gaines running that saloon. He ain't been in town long, but he's sure putting the bite on soldiers. And they decided to put a stop to it. So there was trouble.'

'And that sort of trouble can quickly get out of hand,' Moran mused.

Grimmer nodded. He led the way into the nearest building and opened one of several doors in a long corridor. In the small room that was revealed a single bed stood along the left-hand

13

wall, with a window beside it on the right. A wardrobe occupied most of the opposite wall. In the corner and in front of the window on its left was a washstand with a tall jug filled with water standing beneath it. Moran's travelling trunk was in front of the washstand.

'I've detailed an orderly to take care of you while you're here, Captain. He's Private Sheldon, an old soldier who knows all the ropes, so you'll be made as comfortable as possible. When you're presentable perhaps you'll return to the troop office. Colonel Denton asked me to inform him when you arrived. He's keen to stop the situation from worsening.'

'Give me an hour,' Moran said. 'I'll need to know what fresh orders have arrived for me.'

Grimmer saluted and departed. Moran opened the trunk and laid out his best uniform on the bed. He stripped to the waist, washed, and was donning his uniform when a heavy

hand knocked at the door. He called out an invitation to enter; the door opened, and a tall, thin soldier entered and saluted.

'Private Sheldon — your orderly, sir, reporting for duty,' he said in a clipped tone. 'If you want anything just ask for it, Captain, and I'll get it.'

'Thank you, Sheldon. You can clean my boots for a start. I'm to see the colonel shortly.'

'He's one of the best, sir. He goes by the book, Captain, but he's fair.'

Moran smiled. No soldier worth his salt would bad-mouth one officer to another.

'I heard you brought in Buster Green, Captain. Did he come quietly?'

'He picked up some bruises on the way, but eventually learned to accept his change of fortune.'

'Did he admit to killing Rogers, Captain?'

'I can't comment on that. Tell me about the trouble in town.'

Sheldon shrugged. 'A new gambler

took over in Brannigan's saloon and started cheating bluecoats. That's what started it.'

'And that could blow up into something more serious,' Moran said.

'It's done that already, sir.' Sheldon grimaced. 'Three men roughed up the gambler. They haven't been identified yet. But last night the saloon caught fire, and it's a wonder the whole town wasn't burned down. No one has come out from town yet to accuse soldiers of doing it, but Sheriff Steadman will surely turn up before the day is out.'

'The town is off limits right now, isn't it?'

'It sure is, but that won't stop some of the men from dealing out their own brand of justice. I'll fetch my cleaning gear, sir. I'll be right back.'

Sheldon departed, to return within a few moments. He set to work cleaning Moran's boots whilst giving Moran background information on everyday life at the fort. Moran was almost ready to return to the company office

when a knock at the door interrupted Sheldon's chatter and Top Sergeant Grimmer appeared in the doorway.

'If you're ready, Captain, perhaps you'll come and see the colonel now,' Grimmer said. 'The sheriff has just arrived from town, and Colonel Denton would like you to be present. There was more trouble in the town last night, sir. Brannigan's saloon was damaged by fire. The sheriff says the blaze was started deliberately, and he's got a witness who saw two soldiers running from the area.'

'I'll be along right away,' Moran said, and Grimmer departed. Moran turned to Sheldon. 'How did you know about the fire in town if the sheriff has only just turned up to report it?' he asked.

'No names, no pack drill, Captain.' Sheldon grinned. 'A buzz went round the lines this morning.'

'I understand.' Moran opened the door to leave, and then paused. 'Unpack my gear from the trunk while I'm gone,' he said.

Sheldon nodded. Moran went across to the company office. Top Sergeant Grimmer had preceded him, and was waiting at the door to the colonel's office. He opened the office door, stepped inside, and reported:

'Provost Captain Moran is here, Colonel.' He stepped aside and Moran entered the office.

Colonel Denton was small-boned, his features bronzed, blue eyes glinting with an inner fire. He was in his early fifties. His blue uniform, with its yellow cavalry facings, was immaculate. He arose from his desk and came forward with his right hand outstretched. Moran saluted, and then shook hands.

'I'm glad you've arrived, Captain,' Denton greeted, returning to his seat behind the desk. 'Trouble is descending on us from all quarters. I congratulate you for apprehending Private Green so quickly. Fresh orders have arrived for you from your headquarters. You are to check out this local trouble we're getting. And this is Sheriff Steadman.

He's called this morning to report more trouble involving soldiers in Lodgepole last night.'

Moran turned to the big man seated in front of the desk. Sheriff Steadman was tall, broad-shouldered, and handsome, with rugged features, brown eyes and a shock of black hair that was neatly trimmed. He looked to be about forty years old; was dressed in a light-blue town suit and a string tie. A cartridge belt was buckled around his waist, its holster containing a walnut-handled Colt .45, and the loops in the belt were filled with glinting cartridges. He got to his feet and held out a hand, a smile on his face.

'Glad to know you, Captain,' he greeted. 'I'm sorry to be here with such bad news. I'm trying to get to grips with what's going on in town, but it's getting worse by the day.'

'We'll stamp it out, Sheriff,' Colonel Denton said sharply. 'I suspect that a small group of soldiers is responsible for the outbreak, and they will be

severely dealt with. We do have troublemakers at the fort, but we know who they are. I have given orders for discipline to be enforced, and any man who steps out of line after this will rue the day he was born. Pull up a chair, Captain, and I'll acquaint you with the facts as we know them.'

Moran sat down. Sheriff Steadman leaned back in his chair and spoke in a harsh tone.

'As I was saying, Colonel, I have a witness who saw two soldiers running away from the saloon as the alarm was being raised. They had horses waiting along the street; they mounted up and took out fast in this direction. We were lucky to be able to get the fire under control quickly. Some damage was done to the back of the saloon, but it was not serious, although it could have been a whole lot worse. If it had been the middle of summer the whole town would have burned down. Whoever started the fire sure didn't give a hoot about the folks living there. I can

understand men trying to get their own back on someone who cheated them, but this business last night goes beyond the bounds of righteous anger. It was downright murderous.'

'I agree wholeheartedly, Sheriff.' Colonel Denton nodded. 'Do you have any suspicion of which soldiers have a grievance against that gambler — Elroy Gaines? And is he running crooked games in the saloon?'

'There's no proof of that, Colonel.' Steadman shook his head.

'I'll clamp down on every man on the post,' said Denton fiercely. 'I won't tolerate indiscipline, and if any of my men are responsible for setting fire to the saloon I'll make an example of them.' He studied Moran's intent face for several moments, his blue eyes glinting like shards of broken glass, and then made a visible effort to control his anger. 'I've had good reports of you, Captain, and I hope you'll soon get to grips with this situation.'

'I'll start my investigation immediately, Colonel,' Moran replied, 'and when I have some background knowledge of the situation I'll pull out all the stops.'

'Then I can safely leave the matter in your hands.' Denton arose and reached for his hat. 'Thank you for calling, Sheriff. You can rest assured that no stone will be left unturned, and any of my men found guilty of causing your trouble with be dealt with severely.'

Sheriff Steadman shook hands and departed. Denton heaved a sigh as the office door closed behind the lawman.

'I hope you'll get quick results with your investigation, Captain,' he said. He consulted a pocket watch and nodded. 'I'm holding a parade to read the riot act to the men. I hope it will have a quietening effect on the ranks. Don't hesitate to call on me for help if you need it. Everyone in the fort is at your disposal. You have a free hand, and don't hesitate to use anyone or anything as you may require.'

'Thank you, Colonel. I need to get a statement from Private Green before I do anything else. Then you can proceed with his court martial. I'll need to talk to witnesses, and anyone who may have any knowledge of the murder.'

'All I ask is that you report to me once a day to keep me informed of your progress. I've given an order to Top Sergeant Grimmer to assist you in any way he can. If there is anything I have overlooked then come and tell me.'

Denton strode out of the office and Moran followed him into the outer office. The top sergeant was waiting with a brown folder in his hands, which he handed to Moran.

'This contains names and statements of the men who have some knowledge of what happened the night the sutler was murdered, Captain,' Grimmer said. 'There's nothing conclusive about it. Some men have said they think Green killed Rogers, and others have said the opposite, but you're interested in proof, and apparently there is none.'

23

Moran said: 'I understand that Rogers was stabbed to death.'

'That's right. And I wouldn't expect Green to admit to anything that would put a rope around his neck. Anyway, you'll form your own conclusions after you've been through the file.'

'I'll need an office, or a place to work,' Moran said.

'Feel free to use the desk over there, Captain. It's hardly ever used, except by the duty officer. Perhaps you'll excuse me now, sir. I have to get on parade with Three Troop.'

Grimmer departed and Moran sat down at the desk in the corner. He opened the file and began to read the five statements it contained. One statement, made by a trooper named Hilton, was the only one that seemed to contain an eyewitness report of Green apparently murdering the sutler, but by the end of the statement Hilton seemed to disagree with his own evidence. Two of the other statements merely suggested that Green was the killer, and

the final two statements thought Green was innocent. By the time he had scanned and mentally digested the contents of the folder, Top Sergeant Grimmer was re-entering the office.

'There's nothing hard and fast about who the killer could be except Hilton's statement. Nobody seems to know exactly what took place on the night Rogers was killed,' Moran shook his head. 'It looks bad for Green, I must admit, but he is innocent until proved guilty. I will talk to each of the men listed here, and Trooper Hilton in particular, but first I must get Green's statement down on paper. I saw a statement by Mrs Rogers, the sutler's widow. Is she still at the fort?'

'No, sir, she moved into Lodgepole after Rogers was buried, and as far as I know she's staying in the hotel there. The guardhouse is to the left, at the other end of the porch, sir,' Grimmer added. 'I've had a word with Police Sergeant Buller, and he'll help you any way he can.'

Moran nodded and went out to the porch. He paused for a moment to look around, watched a squad drilling on the parade ground, and then went along the porch to the guardhouse at the far end. A small barred window looked out on to the porch, and beside it a heavy wooden door gave access to the interior. Moran entered and looked around. The guardhouse was gloomy, sparsely furnished, and had a scrubbed look about it which, coupled with a strong smell of disinfectant, gave the place a unique but familiar atmosphere.

A desk was situated beside the window, and a sergeant sprang up from behind it to salute energetically. He was large and powerful. His fleshy face was unattractive, and not enhanced by a scar above his mouth that pulled his lips slightly to the left. His head was covered in stubble cut to less than half an inch, and dark eyes glowered from under bushy black brows. He looked like a wild dog ready to pounce on

anyone who bothered him.

'Police Sergeant Buller, sir,' he rapped. 'One prisoner in the cells, present and correct, Captain.'

'Thank you, Sergeant. I'm Provost Captain Moran. I arrested Green and brought him in. Now I want to get a statement from him. I'll see him in his cell.'

'Yes, sir, if you'll follow me, Captain.'

Sergeant Buller crossed the room and unlocked a door in the back wall which gave access to a short corridor with iron-barred cell doors on either side. He jangled his keys as he walked along the corridor, and when he paused at a cell and peered through the bars before unlocking the door he uttered an exclamation. Moran, startled, hurried forward, looked into the cell, and then rapped:

'Open the door quickly, Sergeant.'

Inside the cell, Private Green was slumped at the barred widow, which was high up in the back wall. Green, his feet clear of the ground, was suspended

27

from a length of cord which was
knotted around his neck; the other end
was fixed securely to a window bar.

2

Sheriff Steadman's thoughts were troubled as he left the fort and rode at a canter on the five-mile trip back to Lodgepole, a cow town with a population of some 500 souls. Having a fort in his bailiwick made life difficult. If the soldiers were not in town at weekends, drinking and causing all kinds of trouble, then they were trying to make out with the local womenfolk, causing a different kind of trouble with husbands or boyfriends. It was a regular feature of Saturday nights: having to haul drunken soldiers into the cells or breaking up brawls, with the occasional gunfight thrown in for good measure. And the trouble was steadily worsening.

Steadman could see which way the wind was blowing, and knew that he had to clamp down on the troublemakers before things really got out of hand.

The signs were there that a real emergency would inevitably crop up, and his worst fear was that lives would be lost, blowing up the situation into a full-scale war between soldiers and townsmen. As he rode he considered the small snippets of information he had picked up about the trouble. There had been a number of complaints about soldiers, and he had been quick to realize that some of the townsmen were at fault — men like Elroy Gaines, the new gambler at Brannigan's saloon.

Gaines was a professional gambler: slick at his job. Steadman, being wise in the ways of such people, had seen him manipulating the cards but had remained silent about the incident. Now, in view of the growing trouble, he realized that he would have to nip the cheating business in the bud. He sighed and urged his horse on at a faster pace, aware that there were others in town who needed to pull in their horns and toe the line, and he knew the time had come for swift action in order stop the

rot before he was overwhelmed.

When he reached Lodgepole and dismounted outside the livery barn he could smell the stink of the fire that had burned the back of Brannigan's saloon the night before. He sighed long and heavily as he permitted his horse to drink from the water trough before leading the animal inside the barn. As he was unsaddling, Otis Jary, the liveryman, emerged from his office and came to the stall where the sheriff was working on his horse. Jary was a small man, middle-aged, slim, and untidy. His clothes needed washing, and a shave would have enhanced his appearance. He drank too much, but caused no trouble in town, and acted as an extra pair of eyes and ears for Steadman, watching points and reporting men for the slightest misdemeanour. Jary glanced around the stable as if afraid of being overheard, and then leaned closer to Steadman, who recoiled from the stink of Jary's unwashed body.

'I gotta tell you, Sheriff,' Jary hissed.

His breath stank of whiskey and he almost fell against Steadman, who fended him off. 'The town is off limits to soldiers, but one rode in a while ago, and he'll be up to no good, I reckon. He's probably showed up to check on the damage done to the saloon last night. You can pick him up at Myron Tate's house. He's the sergeant who's courting Tate's daughter Nora.'

'That's Shiloh Grove, the mail sergeant at the fort,' Steadman replied, shaking his head. 'He comes into town every day. The off-limits order doesn't apply to him. I reckon he's one of the good soldiers. He don't drink and never causes trouble.' Steadman wished all the soldiers would take Sergeant Grove as an example of how to behave. 'Have you heard anything about who might have started the fire last night? Do you know the names of any soldiers who complained about being cheated by Elroy Gaines?'

Jary shrugged. 'It would be easier to tell you who hasn't been cheated by

that no-good cardsharp. Brannigan should know better than to employ such a crooked polecat. Gaines is so crooked he makes a corkscrew look like a new pin. If you don't do something about him, Sheriff, you're gonna get a lot more trouble blowing up in your face.'

'Tell me something I don't know.' Steadman shook his head. He held his breath as Jary exhaled over him and he was enveloped in an invisible cloud of bad breath. He pushed past Jary and headed for the street. 'Finish my horse, Otis,' he growled. 'I'll see you later.'

He gulped a lungful of fresh air and went along the street to Brannigan's saloon. The main street was quiet. It was early afternoon and the town seemed half-asleep. But he heard an insistent hammering in the background and guessed that Will Thomas, the town carpenter, was at work in the saloon, replacing the burnt timbers damaged by the fire. He pushed through the batwings into the saloon. Brannigan,

the owner, was standing behind the long bar, checking some stock sheets, attended as always by Joe Sharkey, the bartender.

Brannigan was short, obese, and dark-haired. His fleshy face was shapeless, with red cheeks and a double chin. His eyes were well back in his head under a high forehead that was accentuated by a receding hairline. He had piglike eyes that were over-bright, filled with an innate cunning that he could not conceal.

Sharkey was a tall beanpole of a man, with blue eyes and fair hair.

'Whiskey, Sheriff?' Sharkey called when he looked up at the sound of the batwings creaking.

Steadman paused and the batwings smacked against his broad shoulders.

'Not right now,' he replied, gazing across the big room at a corner table where four men were playing poker. His eyes narrowed when he saw the tall slim figure of Elroy Gaines sitting with his back to a wall, unsmiling face hawk-like

as he watched the play and the players. Steadman suppressed a flicker of a smile when he saw the livid bruises on Gaines's face, inflicted in the attack by three unknown cavalrymen.

Gaines was in his thirties and dressed like a gambler — black broadcloth town suit, white ruffled shirt and black string tie. He was a handsome man. His eyes were brown and his black hair was greased and plastered down: not a strand out of place. His lithe body was motionless, only his eyes moved, and he had an air about him that reminded Steadman of a rattlesnake ready to strike.

Steadman walked across to the bar to Brannigan, who looked up enquiringly.

'I need to talk to you, Cully,' Steadman said abruptly.

'Sounds like more trouble has come up,' Cully Brannigan observed. 'Do you wanta go into my office?'

'What I have to say is for your ears only,' Steadman countered.

Brannigan nodded, emerged from

behind the bar: and led the way to a door under the stairs which gave access to the upper floor of the saloon. Steadman shook his head when he entered the office. The fire of the previous night had damaged the rear of the office and the hammering was too loud for conversation. Will Thomas was on a ladder outside. There was a hole in the back wall where burned planks had been removed. Thomas looked in and grinned at Steadman.

'We'll have to go out to the main street,' Brannigan said hoarsely.

They went back through the saloon, pushed through the batwings, and walked out to the sidewalk.

'What's on your mind, Pete?' Brannigan demanded.

'I've just got back from the fort,' Steadman said. 'Colonel Denton read the riot act to his men, but that's no guarantee it will stop the trouble. You've got to do something about Gaines, or the next time the soldiers come here they'll surely do a good job on this

place. I've got the smell of bad trouble coming up, so you'd better pull in your horns.'

'I talked to Gaines and he denies cheating.' Brannigan shrugged. 'That's all I can do, unless I actually catch him at it.'

'There's no smoke without fire, and a number of soldiers have complained of the cheating. I saw Gaines palm a card or two the other evening, so I'm inclined to accept the word of the soldiers, and if I get any more complaints I'll come for Gaines. You can bet on it.'

'Why don't you have a word with Gaines yourself?' Brannigan countered.

Steadman studied Brannigan's face for a moment before nodding.

'OK, go back in and tell him to come out here.'

Brannigan turned on his heel and pushed through the batwings. Steadman glanced around the street, his eyes narrowed, his thoughts dark and troubled.

'You wanta see me, Sheriff?' Elroy Gaines pushed through the batwings and confronted Steadman. 'What's wrong?'

'You're what's wrong, Gaines. Stop cheating at the tables.'

'Cheating?' The gambler's expression hardened. His features were misshapen, swollen: his injuries looked painful. His voice soared several notes higher up the scale as he continued: 'What the hell do you mean — cheating?' He gazed at Steadman lopsided, a challenge in his gaze.

'So you're a liar as well as a cheat.' Steadman spoke evenly. 'I saw you palming cards the other evening and overlooked it, but now there's big trouble looming, so cut out the cheating and play it straight from now on — or else.'

'You're mistaken, Sheriff.' Gaines's tone changed again. 'I have never cheated in my life, and I resent being accused of it.'

Steadman's patience fled in the face

38

of the gambler's blatant lie.

'You're a cheap, four-flushing crook,' he rasped. 'And you're stupid with it. I'm warning you to lay off, and I'll be around to make you do as you're told. If I see one more instance of cheating you'll think the roof of the saloon has fallen in on you. I'll bang you in a cell so fast you won't know what time of day it is, and I'll throw away the key. I'm not asking you to stop cheating, I'm telling you. So pay attention and do like I say. No more cheating.'

Gaines stared into Steadman's eyes, a muscle under his half-closed left eye twitching as he considered. Then he nodded and went back into the saloon. Steadman watched the batwings flap to and fro until they stopped moving. Then he released his pent-up breath in a loud sigh and went on to his office, relieved that he had confronted the gambler.

The day jailer, Mike Colton, was seated at Steadman's desk when the

sheriff entered the office. Colton, short and fleshy, was a physical powerhouse. He exercised regularly, and was proud of his strength and fitness. He was a good man in a fight, and dealt fairly with any prisoner who came into his care. Men did not try to take advantage of him. He wore a gunbelt and a holstered pistol. The big ring of his large bunch of cell keys was hung over the flared handle of his Colt .45 and lay against his thick thigh.

'Hi, Sheriff,' Colton greeted when Steadman entered the office. The jailer's voice rumbled out of his barrel-like chest. 'How were things at the fort?'

'Not good, Mike. I think there's big trouble coming. But I'm taking steps to get a grip on the situation around town. I told that damn four-flusher Gaines to stop his cheating.'

'Brannigan should kick him out. I watched Gaines last night. He's good at what he does, but I spotted him forcing cards. And he's fleecing local men.

Brannigan will get a bad name if he don't put a halter on Gaines.'

'That's what I told him. Is Mossley back from the Rafter O yet?'

'I ain't seen hide or hair of him.' Colton grimaced. 'He's had more than enough time to get out there and back. Do you think something might have happened to him?'

'Dick can take care of himself,' Steadman mused. 'I'll give him until tomorrow morning. Chuck Osman might have given him a lead to the horse-thieves. If he ain't back before noon then I'll have to ride out to Rafter O and see what's going on.'

'Stealing horses is getting to be big business,' Colton said. 'All those remounts the army wants. There's a ready market waiting to be supplied.'

'I don't think it's an organized thing.' Steadman shook his head. 'A thief worth his salt wouldn't steal broncs off this range and sell them to the army at Fort Collins.'

'There are plenty other forts out

West,' Colton suggested, 'and nags are easy to move.'

Steadman sighed, jerked his thumb, and Colton arose from the desk. Steadman sat down and tried to relax but failed to find easement. He had a nasty hunch in the back of his mind which was not quite ready to blossom, and as yet he could draw no conclusions from his unaccountable uneasiness. But hard experience had him feeling as uneasy as a dog with fleas, and he could only suffer in silence while the situation worsened.

★ ★ ★

Moran dashed into the cell, seized Green's inert body, and supported the dead weight of the senseless man in an attempt to take the pressure off his neck.

'Quick, cut the cord,' he rapped.

The provost sergeant pulled a clasp knife from a pocket, opened it, and slashed the cord with a quick motion.

Moran lowered Green to the floor and Buller pulled the cord from around the limp neck. Moran pressed a hand against Green's chest and then sighed heavily. There was no heartbeat.

'He's dead,' Moran said. 'There'll be hell to pay over this, Sergeant. Where did he get the cord from? Did you carry out a full body search when he was brought in?'

'I wasn't on duty then, Captain,' Buller replied. 'When I relieved Corporal Bessey, Green was already in this cell, and I assumed that all the checks had been carried out when he was received.'

Moran stood up, his gaze on the dead soldier's face. 'Get Corporal Bessey back here,' he rapped. 'And while you're at it, tell Top Sergeant Grimmer what's happened.'

Buller departed at a run. Moran went out to the front office and sat down at the desk, his mind alive with conjecture. Green hadn't seemed suicidal. Moran opened the folder Grimmer had

given him and looked again at the five statements collected from men who had some knowledge of the events of the night the sutler was killed. He found Corporal Bessey's name on the list and read the statement Bessey had made at the original inquiry into the events surrounding the murder. Bessey had been in the store when Green entered, and had heard an altercation between Green and the sutler. Green had asked for credit and Rogers had refused. An argument had developed during which Rogers ordered Green to leave the store. Green had uttered threats as he departed. It was alleged that Green returned later to steal two bottles of whiskey, had been disturbed by Rogers, and stabbed the sutler.

Sergeant Buller returned, followed by a tall, lean individual who gazed at Moran with shock and disbelief in his narrowed eyes.

'Corporal Bessey, Captain,' Buller reported.

'So what happened when Green was brought in, Corporal?' Moran demanded.

'I carried out the usual routine for admitting a prisoner into detention, sir,' Bessey replied in a clipped tone. 'He stripped and was searched. Any items which could have been used to harm himself were removed, Captain. I made a list of his belongings. He had next to nothing on him.'

'Were you alone with the prisoner when he was brought in?' Moran asked.

'No, sir. Private Johnson of the police squad was on duty. He carried out the search under my supervision, sir.'

'I'll want to talk to Johnson now, Sergeant,' Moran rapped.

Sergeant Buller hurried away.

'Stand at ease, Corporal,' Moran ordered, and Bessey relaxed.

'I've read the preliminary inquiry into the murder of Rogers, the post sutler, and your name is on the list of witnesses. Have you anything to add to the statement you made?'

'No, sir. I reported fully on what I saw and heard.'

'You knew Green well, I take it. What kind of a soldier was he?'

'He was average, sir — performed his duties and gave no trouble.'

'Were you friendly with him?'

'There was no reason not to be, sir. He never complained and always obeyed orders efficiently. He was reliable, Captain. I would have trusted him with my life.'

Sergeant Buller returned with a clattering of boots on the wooden floor, accompanied by Private Johnson.

'That will be all for now, Corporal,' Moran said, and Bessey departed.

Johnson was an older soldier, in his thirties. He stood to attention, gazing unfocused with unblinking brown eyes at an imaginary spot on the wall behind Moran's head. Sergeant Buller stood motionless beside the desk, watching Johnson intently.

'You were present when Private Green was brought into the cells, Johnson?'

'Yes, sir. I was on duty with Corporal Bessey. We went off duty shortly after Green came in, when Sergeant Buller took over.'

'You carried out the search on Green?'

'Yes, sir, in accordance with standing orders for handling the admission of prisoners, Captain.'

'And then Green was locked in a cell. Was he checked after that?'

'I looked in on him once before going off duty, sir.' Johnson's tone was low and tense. 'That would be about twenty minutes after he was locked in. I went off duty fifteen minutes after that, when Sergeant Buller took over.'

'And when you took over, Sergeant, did you check on Green at all?'

'Yes, Captain. It was the first thing I did when I came on duty. It's in regulations, sir. I entered Green's cell to check him, and asked if he had any complaints. He replied in the negative, sir. I assessed his manner, which was calm. He did not seem unduly

depressed beyond what would be expected of a man returning to his unit faced with a charge of murder. I always check on new prisoners every thirty minutes, Captain.'

'So how did Green get hold of the cord he used to hang himself?' Moran mused.

'I have no idea, sir,' Buller replied.

'It's the first question that will be asked at the inquiry,' Moran said, 'and we must have the answer. It's obvious Green didn't bring the cord into the guardhouse when he was admitted, and the alternative is that someone gave it to him.'

'Or it was in the cell when he entered it, sir,' Buller suggested with a shrug.

'That's hardly likely, is it?' Moran shook his head.

'If we're looking for possible ways the cord might have got into the cell then the only other explanation is that one of the police on duty gave it to him,' Johnson observed.

'I was coming to that,' Moran rasped.

'Did you give the cord to the prisoner, Johnson?'

'No, sir, I wouldn't have done that even if Green had asked me to get it for him. It didn't cross my mind that he would want to end his life, Captain, because I don't believe he murdered the sutler, sir.'

'Have you any reason for thinking that?' Moran demanded.

'No, sir.' Johnson shook his head emphatically.

The door opened and Top Sergeant Grimmer entered the guardroom. He saluted and came to stand beside Johnson.

'This is a bad business,' sir,' Grimmer said. 'Have you any idea what happened?'

'Not at the moment.' Moran got to his feet. 'I'll talk to the colonel again.'

'Colonel Denton has left the fort to visit Lodgepole, sir. He wants to check on the town and see for himself what has been happening there. If there's anything you need, sir, you have only to

ask. I have orders to assist you in any way that's possible, Captain.'

'I must ride into Lodgepole as soon as possible if I'm to carry out an investigation into the trouble.' Moran got to his feet. 'I'll change out of uniform to make my visit. Soldiers won't be a welcome sight in town at this time, and I need to move around freely and talk to people.'

'I'll get the post surgeon to examine Green, Captain,' Sergeant Buller said.

'And try to discover how Green got hold of that cord,' Moran replied.

He left the guardhouse and went back to his quarters, changed out of uniform, and prepared to visit Lodgepole. His horse was in a corral in the horse lines; he saddled up and rode to the troop office to see Top Sergeant Grimmer.

'I'm going into town to look around and get some idea of what's been going on there,' he told Grimmer. 'Tell me what's happened to the three soldiers who beat up the gambler. I didn't see

them in the guardhouse.'

'They're under open arrest, Captain. The colonel has gone into Lodgepole to talk to the gambler who was attacked, and when he returns the three will be sentenced.'

'The sutler, Rogers,' Moran said. 'Where is his widow now?'

Her name is Helen Rogers. She lived with Rogers in an apartment over the trading post. After the murder she moved into town, and I believe she's still there, staying at the hotel.'

'I'll drop in and talk to her,' Moran mused. 'I'll be back later.'

Moran went out to his horse, swung into the saddle and left the fort. He followed the well-beaten trail to town, riding easily, his keen eyes shadowed by the brim of his Stetson. He checked his surroundings instinctively from long habit, and was probably two miles from the fort when he heard the rolling echoes of a shot, coming from the direction of the town. He touched spurs to his mount and went forward at a

gallop, aware that Colonel Denton was somewhere ahead.

More shots sounded, and Moran pushed his horse into greater effort. The trail twisted and turned, bypassing clusters of grey rocks. He reached for his holstered pistol, for the shooting was close, and eventually came across a saddle horse standing in the cover of rocks. He glanced around quickly, and saw a puff of gun smoke rising from cover to his left. He caught a glimpse of a blue uniform, and saw the barrel of a rifle poking out of the scant cover.

A bullet crackled in Moran's left ear. He dismounted swiftly and trailed his reins, grabbed his rifle from its saddle boot, and dived into cover. He worked his way to where Colonel Denton was crouching behind a rock. The colonel had removed his hat. Sweat was beading his rugged forehead. He glanced at Moran and smiled and nodded, paused, and fired a shot. He returned his attention to Moran.

'Glad to see you, Captain. There are

two men ahead. They ambushed me; opened fire without warning. I have no idea who they are, but obviously they don't like soldiers. If you'll engage them from here I'll go forward and get to closer quarters.'

'It might be better if you remained here, Colonel, and let me check on them,' Moran replied. 'I'm accustomed to situations such as this.'

'Don't take any undue risks,' Denton replied. He lifted his rifle and fired again.

Moran moved out, circled to the left, and crawled through the scattered rocks towards the sound of the return fire. He could make out two weapons shooting at the colonel, and eased out further to his left. With any luck he might take a prisoner and gain some valuable knowledge of the local situation.

3

Elroy Gaines confronted Brannigan when he left Sheriff Steadman outside the saloon, his bruised face suffused with anger. Brannigan grinned when he saw the gambler's discomfiture. He moved out from behind the bar, motioned for Gaines to accompany him, and walked across the saloon away from the bar.

'Hell,' Brannigan rasped, 'that damned hammering is sending me crazy. There ain't no rest from it. Why in hell did you start cheating, Elroy? Ain't we got enough trouble without you adding to it?' He paused and studied the bruises on the gambler's face. 'Didn't the soldiers teach you not to play tricks when they're in a game? And Steadman laid down the law, huh? Take my advice and do like he says. He's no pushover. He'll watch

you now, and if you take one step out of line he'll fall on you like a wagonload of fence posts.'

'You'd better find someone to take the shine off his badge,' Gaines rasped. 'It's not good to have a lawman against you. You must know someone who will put him away for a few dollars.'

'Are you loco?' Brannigan grimaced. 'Sure I can find someone to do the job, but if we get rid of him the next sheriff might be even worse. We'll stick with him and see how it turns out. Jake Woodson will be around pretty soon now. He's setting himself up on a derelict horse ranch out by Owl Creek, and when he starts operating, your penny-ante card tricks won't be worth the bother. Clean up your act, Elroy, and do it as of now. I don't want any more aggravation with soldiers. They're here to stay and we've got to live with that. The sooner you realize that the better for all concerned.'

'Can you trust Woodson to do the

job the way you want it?' Gaines demanded.

'I trust him like I trust my own mother.' Brannigan grinned. 'Woody has been a horse-thief ever since he crawled out of his cradle. He'll clean out this range with no trouble.'

Gaines shook his head. 'I don't like the sound of that deal,' he said.

'You don't have to like it. All you've got to do is run a straight game and keep everyone happy. Look at the trouble I've got now because you didn't do it right. I damned near lost the saloon last night and all because you couldn't do like you're told and play it straight. If I catch you trying anything else crooked you'll have me climbing on your back. I have to go to the bank right now and beg a loan off that long-nosed Myron Tate. He'll skin me alive if he agrees the loan, but he won't like lending dough to the likes of me.'

Gaines cursed and turned away, not liking the situation. He went back to his

game of poker, but his mind was not on it, and his thoughts were far ranging as he considered the situation. He was not happy about being involved in the scheme in which Brannigan planned to steal horses for sale to the army, especially when it would involve shooting and killing, and he wondered if he should cut his losses and get out while he could. He decided to postpone a decision, concentrated on the poker game in progress, and could not refrain from cheating a little. Hell, he thought, a gambler had to keep practising his dubious art!

Brannigan walked back behind the bar and stood watching Gaines for several minutes. He glanced at Sharkey, who was working on the inventory, and sighed heavily. He needed to get away from the saloon for a spell.

'Joe, I've got to see Tate at the bank. I'll be back later. Keep an eye on things, huh?'

'Sure thing, boss,' Sharkey replied.

Brannigan left the saloon.

Sergeant Dave Grove, nicknamed 'Shiloh' because he had participated in that particular battle in the Civil War, was mail sergeant at the fort, and the off-limits order affecting the soldiers did not apply to him. He had to ride into town each day to meet the stagecoach and collect any mail for the fort. During his regular visits to Lodgepole he met Nora, the daughter of the local banker, Myron Tate, and had fallen in love with her. But he did not like her father, who left much to be desired both in looks and manner. Grove wanted to marry Nora, and planned to remove her from her father's sphere of influence as soon as possible after their marriage, which, in his estimation, could not come soon enough.

When he rode into town on the day after the attempted burning of Brannigan's saloon he noticed a difference in the atmosphere as he awaited the

arrival of the westbound Wells Fargo coach. The townsmen with whom he usually came into contact were distant in manner. Grove had not heard about the arson attack on Brannigan's saloon, and was shocked when he was acquainted with the fact. He denied that soldiers were responsible, and was filled with disquiet when he learned that two soldiers had been seen running away from the saloon. When the stage arrived, he collected a mailbag addressed to the fort and rode to the smart house in the residential part of town where Nora lived with her banker father.

Nora was a tall, slim girl in her middle twenties, a red-haired beauty with blue eyes, and she was deeply in love with Grove. But her face exhibited a troubled expression when she greeted him, and Grove felt concerned when he saw her.

'What's wrong, Nora?' he asked, assuming that she was perturbed by the arson attack on the saloon.

'My father has told me to stop seeing you, Dave,' she replied. 'Soldiers are bad news in town now, and you know what my father is like. The slightest breath of trouble or scandal and he erupts. A man was beaten up by soldiers a few days ago, and last night two soldiers tried to burn down the saloon. It's a wonder the whole town didn't go up in flames.'

'It's a bad business,' Grove agreed. 'But the man who was beaten was a gambler at the saloon, and he had been caught cheating soldiers. So why hasn't your father put the blame where it belongs? The gambler should have been ridden out of town on a rail, and tarred and feathered. And I wasn't involved in the trouble, so why does your pa pick on me?'

'You're wearing a uniform,' she replied. 'Father says all soldiers are tarred with the same brush.'

'And he wants you to stop seeing me.' Grove shook his head. 'I'm getting a mite sick of the way your father treats

you, Nora. He's a bully.'

'He's my father, and I cannot disobey him while I live under his roof.' She sighed and tears filled her eyes. 'I think it would be for the best if we do not see each other for a week or so, until the trouble in town dies down. Then we can go ahead with our plans.'

'I don't like giving way to your father,' he responded. 'I've a good mind to go along to the bank and straight talk to him.'

Nora looked at him with horror in her eyes. 'Please don't even consider it, Dave,' she pleaded. 'That's the worst thing you could do. You need to keep a low profile for a few days. Please do it my way or you'll add to the problems facing us.'

'I'm always bending over backwards where your father is concerned,' Grove said wearily. 'There'll have to be some changes after we're married, Nora.'

'Let's do it right or we'll never make it to the church,' she replied.

Grove heaved a sigh and took her

into his arms. 'I'll do like you say,' he muttered. 'I always do.'

* * *

Brannigan walked to the bank and entered. There were no other customers at that moment. He crossed to the counter and paused at the cage where the teller, Humphrey Cole, was seated. Cole looked up from a ledger he was scanning. He was short and fleshy, his brown eyes gleaming behind small round spectacles.

'Mr Brannigan,' he observed. 'I don't see you in here very often. How can I help you?'

'I need to see Tate. He's the one around here with all the money.'

'It was a bad business about the fire at your place last night,' Cole said.

'It could have been a whole lot worse,' Brannigan observed. 'Is Tate in?'

'Yes. I'll tell him you're here.'

Cole got off his stool, crossed to a door in the back wall, tapped on it and

disappeared into Myron Tate's office. Brannigan stood waiting impatiently, looking around with unfocused gaze. Cole reappeared in the doorway and beckoned him.

'Mr Tate will see you,' Cole said. Brannigan passed him and entered the office.

Brannigan swallowed the dislike he felt for Tate as he entered the inner sanctum. The office was large and starkly furnished. There was a small carpet on the floor in front of the big desk, but no curtains at the tall window overlooking the back lots. Tate was seated hunch-shouldered behind his desk. He was small and pale faced, a man who spent most of his waking hours out of the sun. His face was not attractive, with his overlong, pointed nose dominating his features. His mouth resembled a rat trap; thin and uncompromising, its muscles were habitually compressed to keep the lips firm against his teeth. His small eyes were set close together under a broad

forehead, and showed no emotion as he gazed at Brannigan as if the saloon man had crawled out from under a rock. 'You've come about the fire, I suppose,' Tate observed in a dry, crackling voice.

'You've guessed right,' Brannigan replied. 'I'll need at least a thousand bucks to repair the damage.'

'I've already considered the possibility of loaning you the cost of the repairs and I've decided that it would not be in the best interests of the bank to do so. If those soldiers come back to finish the job they started last night then the bank will show a loss.'

'You own half the saloon,' Brannigan said sharply.

'It's your half that was damaged.' Tate laughed in a high-pitched tone.

'Is that supposed to be funny?' Brannigan scowled. 'Remind me to laugh when you loan me the dough.'

'The damage resulted from your bad management.'

'How do you get that?'

'You hired a gambler who was caught

cheating, and then you failed to handle the complaints satisfactorily. Is the gambler still working for you?'

'I need him for another of my business ventures which is starting up shortly. I've warned him against cheating again.'

'What new venture? You haven't been in to discuss it with me.'

'I'll talk to you when I've discovered if it will work or not,' Brannigan kept his dislike for Tate out of his voice and expression.

'What will it cost to set up?' Tate's business acumen instinctively raised its head.

'Nothing from me. I've got a new partner coming into the county and he's handling the money side.'

'Will it be legal?'

'The hell it will! All the legal dough in Morgan County is already tied up. I've got to go into crime to make an honest buck.'

'Take it from me, all money is honest. It's the men who handle it who are not.

How far are you prepared to go to make money?' Tate leaned forward, his head on one side as he gazed intently at Brannigan.

'How far is how far?' Brannigan countered. 'I'll go as far as it takes to make a few dollars.' He laughed. 'Have you got something in mind?'

'Sure: robbing this bank.' Tate smiled at the expression which came to Brannigan's face.

'You've got to be kidding!' Brannigan got to his feet, shaking his head.

'I've been thinking about it for a long, long time.'

'You'd need a gang,' Brannigan mused, 'six men at least. If you are serious then I know just the men for the job. Convince me that this is not some kind of a joke and I'll have them in town in a few days.'

'It's far from being a joke. Sit down again and pin your ears back.' Tate leaned forward in his seat and fixed Brannigan with an unblinking gaze. 'There'll be no shooting, so no one will

get hurt. Your men will come into the bank, pick up the dough, knock me down and leave quietly and quickly. When they are well on their way out of town I'll raise the alarm by firing a shot, and they'll be long gone before anyone can do anything about it.'

Brannigan sat down, suddenly interested, and Tate explained the scheme he had long contemplated.

* * *

Moran worked his way through the rocks towards the spot from where shots were being fired at Colonel Denton. The echoes of the shooting sounded muted in the distance. He pinpointed the area and closed in, holding his fire even when he caught a glimpse of the two men doing the shooting. Colonel Denton was no longer replying to the fire being directed at him, and Moran began to fear that his superior had been shot.

He edged past the position of the two

men, circling and easing to his left, and when the ambushers realized that their victim was no longer resisting they moved forward from their cover and began to close in. Moran halted and raised his rifle. Two men dressed in range clothes drew into his sights and he fired rapidly, triggering a shot at the nearer man and switching his aim without pause. Both men went down almost together, dropping their weapons as hot lead found their flesh. The gun echoes faded rapidly and Moran got to his feet, his deadly rifle ready for further action.

The two men were inert. One was obviously dead, his shirt front bloody with his life blood: a bullet had pierced his heart. The second man was lying on his face, his shoulders heaving with the effort of drawing air into a shattered lung. Moran removed their fallen weapons and then checked them over. He called to the colonel, and when his superior did not respond he went back to where Denton was lying. The colonel

was dead — a red splotch of blood oozing from the bullet hole drilled between his eyes.

Moran heaved a sigh and returned to the wounded man, only to find that he had expired. He crouched beside the man and searched his pockets; he found nothing to identify the corpse. Passing on to the second man he discovered a letter addressed to John Benn, Lodgepole, Colorado. He tucked the letter into his breast pocket and returned to his horse, leaving the grim scene exactly as it was and deciding to fetch the sheriff.

He rode on to town, following the well-defined trail, and cantered into the main street around noon. Lodgepole was a small community, its business premises crowded together on either side of the trail that led eventually to Denver, and it was overlooked by high rocky peaks, some of them snow-capped. Moran saw a sign indicating the position of the law office and dismounted in front of the half-open

door. He dismounted, wrapped his reins around a hitch rail, and stepped up on to the sidewalk. He pushed open the street door and peered into the sparsely furnished office.

Sheriff Steadman was seated at a desk pushed against the left-hand wall under an alley window. A gun rack containing an assortment of rifles and shotguns was on the wall above his head. A row of Wanted dodgers was fastened to the wall, hard eyes gazing from them. Moran entered. Steadman looked up at the sound of Moran's boots, and got to his feet.

'Captain Moran, I didn't expect to see you again so soon,' Steadman greeted with a smile. 'What can I do for you?'

The sheriff's face sobered when Moran explained the purpose for his visit.

'The hell you say!' he exclaimed. 'Can you describe the men you killed?'

'I can do better than that,' Moran said, producing the letter he had found

on one of the men and handing it over.

'John Benn!' Steadman looked up from perusing the envelope and gazed into Moran's steady eyes. 'He hangs out in Brannigan's saloon mostly — one step above being a vagrant. He does odd jobs for Brannigan, and that's how he keeps his head above water. I would have moved him on a long time ago but Brannigan keeps him busy. I've always had my doubts about him.'

'I'll have to ride back to Fort Collins and report Colonel Denton's death,' Moran said. 'If you'll come along I'll show you where the shooting took place and talk you through what happened. I'll give you a statement when I return to town later.'

'Fine. I'll get my horse.'

Moran walked his horse along the street to the livery barn, accompanied by the sheriff. He allowed his mount to drink at the trough near the front door of the barn while Steadman entered to saddle his horse. When they rode out on the trail to the fort Moran filled

71

Steadman in on more details.

'I'd like to look around your town without being identified as a soldier,' Moran said. 'I need to check out a few things, and I'll manage it much better if folks aren't aware that I'm a bluecoat.'

'That's all right by me,' Steadman said easily. 'The trouble started in Brannigan's saloon. I've talked to Brannigan and the gambler who cheated the soldiers. It won't happen again, I can assure you. But it won't be easy to defuse the situation. That fire last night has upset a lot of the townsfolk. It's the worst thing that can happen in a town, and the soldiers responsible for the blaze would have known that.'

'If I catch whoever is responsible they'll go behind bars for a long, long time,' Moran promised.

When they reached the scene of the ambush Moran remained beside the colonel's body while Steadman looked around the area. The sheriff came back to Moran after checking on the two dead ambushers.

'One of them is John Benn,' Steadman said. 'He's the smaller of the two. The other is Adam Pyke. Like I said, Benn works for Brannigan. Pyke is one of the town's carpenters.' Steadman's eyes gleamed. 'I shall want to know why those two were out here ambushing a soldier. I've got it pegged that all the trouble we've had has come from the saloon, and now this has happened, and one of the killers works for Cully Brannigan. It looks like someone is deliberately stirring up more trouble between the soldiers and the town.'

'No one could benefit from such a situation,' Moran mused. He turned his head when he heard the sound of hoofs on the trail, and ran through the rocks to see who was coming. He saw a uniform, and called to the soldier, who was approaching from the town.

'Over here, Sergeant,' Moran called. The sergeant turned his horse obediently and approached. 'I'm Provost Captain Moran. Who are you?'

'Sergeant Grove, sir. I'm mail sergeant at the fort. I've been into town to collect the day's delivery of mail from the East, Captain.'

'There's been a shooting here. Colonel Denton was on his way to town when he was ambushed and killed. The sheriff is here. I want you to report the incident to Top Sergeant Grimmer at the fort, and get a wagon sent out for the colonel's body. Tell Grimmer I'll be back from town later.'

Sergeant Grove was shocked by the news, but said nothing. Moran led the way back to the colonel's body. Sheriff Steadman was loading the bodies of Benn and Pyke on to their horses. Sergeant Grove gazed in shock at Colonel Denton's lifeless body.

'You can ride on to the fort now, Sergeant,' Moran told him. 'Have a detail sent out here as quickly as possible.'

Grove saluted, swung his horse around, and set off at a canter in the direction of the fort. Steadman finished

his grim task, linked the two horses together with their reins, and stepped up into his saddle. He led the way back to town. Moran was thoughtful on the ride, wondering at the trouble that was piling up. When they reached Lodgepole the sheriff rode directly to the law office; several townsmen followed along the sidewalk.

'Who you got there, Sheriff?' someone called.

Steadman ignored the question, and the townsmen gathered around when the sheriff dismounted outside his office.

'Someone can fetch Joe Hiram,' Steadman ordered. 'Tell him there are a couple of bodies for him.'

A townsman went off along the sidewalk.

'Will you accompany me?' Steadman looked at Moran. 'I want to talk to Brannigan about Benn. With any luck we can nip this trouble in the bud.'

'Sure,' Moran said. 'It will be down to me to investigate the colonel's

murder, and it will save time if we do this together.'

They left the growing crowd surrounding the dead men and walked along the sidewalk to the saloon. Steadman pushed through the batwings and Moran followed closely. The sheriff went to the bar, where Brannigan was standing with three men, who were range-dressed and armed. Brannigan was talking loudly and fast, as if he was giving instructions to the men, and the saloon owner broke off when he saw the sheriff.

'Something you want, Sheriff?' Brannigan demanded.

'I want to talk to you when you've got the time,' Steadman replied.

'Not more trouble, I hope,' Brannigan said. He lifted his hands wearily to his shoulders and let them fall back to his sides. 'There's nothing but trouble these days.'

Moran remained several paces behind the sheriff, prepared to be a bystander at this stage of the inquiry.

He looked over the three men with Brannigan, who seemed startled by the sheriff's appearance. One was a tall, burly man wearing twin pistols on crossed cartridge belts, his holsters tied down. Silver hair showed at the nape of his neck although he did not appear to be above the middle thirties. His Stetson was pulled low over his eyes, and his face was weathered, handsome, but wore a taut expression that pulled his lips into a thin line, as if he had been born bad-tempered. His blue eyes were hard and cold, alert and watchful, denoting a man who had a lot of enemies and fully expected them to jump him without warning.

The other two men were alert to their surroundings, and Moran gained the impression that here were men who lived outside the law and were geared to the grim fact that every honest man was against them. All three men glanced at Moran, and one of them reacted instantly. He uttered a curse, swung to

face Moran, and reached for his holstered gun in a fast draw. Moran's own reaction was triggered by his fighting instincts. He set his right hand into motion and grasped the butt of his gun.

4

Moran was lightning fast. The stranger had the edge, and his gun cleared leather and flipped up to line on Moran, who moved like quicksilver. He drew fast; his thumb cocking the weapon as it lifted clear of leather, and he was a split second ahead of his adversary as the foresight covered the other's chest. Moran squeezed his trigger and the pistol erupted flame and smoke. The .45 bullet hammered into the man's sternum and blasted through his heart. The man jerked, lost his grip on his own gun, which clattered to the floor, and as the first echo of the shot thundered across the saloon he went over backwards and followed the gun to the pine boards. A trickle of blood began to form a gory rivulet on the left side of his inert body.

Moran stopped his movement and

stood with his gun covering the other two men, who gazed at him in shock. Nobody moved. The ensuing silence was heavy. Tense seconds ticked by before Steadman cleared his throat and broke the silence.

'He pulled his gun first,' the sheriff said huskily. 'I reckon he knew you from somewhere and figured to get in first.'

'I can't place him,' Moran replied, looking at the upturned face. He shifted his gaze to the silver-haired man. 'It looked like he was with you, so who is he?'

'Walt Gann,' He came to my place a week ago asking for a job, and seemed to know a lot about horses, so I gave him a start.'

'And who are you?' Steadman demanded. 'I ain't seen you before. Have you got a place around here somewhere that I don't know about?'

'I took over a derelict spread north of here, running horses. I'm Jake Woodson, Sheriff. I reckon to sell mounts to

the army. There seems to be a gap in the market which I hope to fill.' He glanced at his motionless companion. 'This is my ranch foreman, Del Manning.'

'What derelict place?' Steadman demanded.

'It's the old Manson spread on Owl Creek, Sheriff,' Brannigan cut in. 'Woodson was just telling me about it.'

'I checked out the place with Amos, the lawyer,' Woodson added. 'He gave me clearance.'

Moran holstered his gun and bent to study Gann's face, searching his memory for details. He nodded slowly.

'He's a deserter from the army,' he told Steadman. 'I ran across him last year but he eluded me. He must have thought I had caught up with him again. I'll send his details to headquarters.'

'We'd better be on our way,' Woodson said. 'Come on, Del, let's head back to the spread. There's work to be done.'

'I'll be out your way to take a look

around,' Steadman said.

'Be glad to see you, Sheriff,' Woodson replied. He and Manning departed.

'So what do you want to talk to me about, Sheriff?' Brannigan asked.

'John Benn.' Steadman replied.

'What about him?'

'He's lying face down across his saddle outside the law office,' Steadman continued. 'He was killed earlier today. He had Adam Pyke with him. They ambushed and killed Colonel Denton, who was on his way to town from the fort.'

Moran, watching Brannigan, saw shock suffuse the saloon man's face, and figured the emotion was genuine. Brannigan put an elbow on the bar and leaned his weight on it.

'I don't believe it,' he said. 'Are you sure Benn did it?'

'When did you last see him?' Steadman countered.

'He was in here at daybreak, cleaning the place, and left as usual to get his breakfast, but he didn't come back at

noon. I was wondering where he'd got to. Now I know.'

'Did he act any different from his normal day?' Steadman asked.

'You mean did he look like a man who was going out this morning to shoot someone.' Brannigan shook his head. 'No, he didn't act any way but normal. He didn't tell me he was planning to ride out and murder the colonel.'

'I don't like the tone in your voice,' Moran said.

'I'm shocked,' Brannigan responded. 'I don't know what I'm thinking or saying right now. I don't need trouble between the soldiers and the town. It ain't good for business. Who are you, anyway? I haven't seen you around.'

'I'm Provost Captain Moran, and I'm here to investigate the trouble you mentioned.' Moran realized that he could not keep his identity a secret.

'Well, I can't help you.' Brannigan shook his head. 'I'm in the middle of this trouble through no fault of my

own. The saloon was almost burned down last night. I hope you can find those responsible.'

'I'll send Hiram in for Gann,' Steadman said. 'I'll talk to you again later, Brannigan.'

Moran followed the sheriff out to the street. Steadman paused on the boardwalk and looked around.

'I'm short-handed at the moment,' he said. 'Dick Mossley, my deputy, rode out yesterday to check on a report of horse stealing. He should have come back by now but he ain't showed, and I'm getting a mite worried about him. I'll have to ride out to the Rafter O later and see if he's there. I know he's sweet on Tilda Osman, Chuck Osman's daughter, but he should have returned right away. Now I want to talk to Otis Jary, the liveryman. Come with me. You'll need to know the background of what's going on.'

Moran nodded. He looked around the street as they went towards the stable. He saw Woodson and Manning

riding out of town, and watched them for a moment, his expression bleak. He saw a group of men coming towards the saloon, attracted by the shooting, and felt a strand of impatience spreading through his mind. He needed to push on and make things happen or he would waste a lot of time getting to grips with the wrongdoers. He had a dead soldier back at the fort and a mystery there to solve. How had Green got hold of the rope with which he hanged himself?

Otis Jary, the liveryman, was standing in the open doorway to his barn, peering along the street in the direction of the saloon. Steadman moved into an upwind position; and Moran, who soon caught the drift of Jary's body odour, did the same.

'Did someone get killed in the saloon?' Jary demanded.

Steadman ignored the question. 'Did you see John Benn ride out of town earlier this morning, Otis?'

'Yeah, said he was gonna visit Abel

Paxton. I ain't seen him come back yet.'

'Did he ride alone?'

'Sure.'

'What was he like when you saw him? Did he seem nervous or fired up about something?'

'He didn't seem different from any other time. He was a man of few words. Is something wrong? Why are you asking about him?'

'I'm just checking out a few facts.' Steadman's tone was quiet and casual. 'Tell me about Adam Pyke. What time did he ride out this morning?'

'Lemme see. He rented a horse and headed out for Frank Saul's spread. He reckons he's got a load of work to do out there. He made an early start — hit the trail around eight.'

'Did Benn and Pyke ride out together?'

'How could they? Benn went north and Pyke rode south. You know that, Sheriff. What are you trying to do — catch me out?'

Steadman remained silent, aware that

he would glean nothing more from the liveryman. He turned to leave. Moran had listened with rising impatience, feeling he was wasting his time. He wanted to get back to the saloon and ask Brannigan some questions but stayed at Steadman's side as they left the barn.

'I need to ride out of town,' Steadman mused. 'I'm real worried about my deputy. It ain't like him to waste time.'

'I'll stick around here,' Moran said.

They went back along the street and Moran turned into the saloon. Half a dozen townsmen were standing at the bar and Brannigan was with them, talking about Colonel Denton's murder. Moran noted that the body of Walt Gann had been removed and sawdust had been applied liberally to the bloodstain. He approached the bar and Brannigan turned to him.

'When are you gonna let the soldiers back into town?' he demanded. 'The off-limits order is killing my business.'

'It wouldn't have come into force if your gambler hadn't been careless and allowed himself to get caught cheating,' Moran countered.

'He won't do that again.' Brannigan shrugged. 'I've always run straight games in here. You can ask anyone in town. No one has ever been cheated.'

There was a murmur of agreement among the townsmen.

'Only soldiers,' Moran mused.

'We don't need soldiers around here,' someone said. 'They bring nothing but trouble — always getting drunk and fighting. And they got no respect for our womenfolk.'

'That's a matter for your sheriff to handle. Soldiers are rough men, but they spend a lot of money around here.' Moran kept his tone neutral, wanting to draw out the opinions of these men.

'It's OK for men like Brannigan,' another said. 'Soldiers only spend money on likker and gambling, and sometimes they cause mayhem in the saloon. But when they spill out into the

town they pick on innocent folk, and the law ain't able to control them. Some get jailed, but those that get away with their bad behaviour keep coming back for more. Townsmen are being beaten up and injured, and it ain't safe for women and children to go out on the street.'

Other men began to voice their opinions, and Moran listened. Complaints against soldiers were nothing new; although the majority of military men were law-abiding, but all shouldered the blame for a minority who had no respect for anyone. Military police patrols were an effective answer, and Moran made a note to check on local conditions.

'If you're a soldier then why are you allowed to come into town with an off-limits rule in force?' The speaker was an older man, well-dressed and obviously prominent in the hierarchy of the community. He was short and fleshy, his cheeks puffed out, his dark eyes filled with aggression. 'I'm Byron

Slessor. I own the hotel, and I'm mayor of this burg.'

'I've just arrived in the area to sort out the trouble,' Moran replied. 'I'm a provost captain, and I'm working with your sheriff to bring order back to the town.'

'I never had much luck with Colonel Denton,' Slessor said. 'I've been riding out to the fort nigh every week with complaints about the behaviour of certain soldiers, but to no avail. And this week, with the off-limits rule in effect, a townsman was beaten up quite badly and an attempt was made to burn down the saloon.'

'I'm looking into the matter,' Moran said keenly. 'Colonel Denton's murder has thrown a great tension into the situation. The two men responsible are dead, but that doesn't clear up the trouble or point to the reason why such drastic action was taken.'

'We're all shocked by the colonel's death.' Slessor shook his head. 'I'm sure Sheriff Steadman will get to the bottom

of the affair, and then perhaps we can all get back to normal. Everyone in town will help you in your job, Captain. We are law-abiding people, and expect visitors to the town to live by our rules.'

'If you mean that then you should have insisted that the crooked gambler was fired from his job and run out of town,' said Moran, his gaze on Brannigan. 'Why haven't you made an example of him to show that you are serious in your wish to overcome the trouble? Goodwill is important in a situation such as you have here.'

Brannigan sighed and shook his head. 'I'll give some thought to what you say,' he said. 'But good gamblers are hard to come by.'

'The gambler you have is obviously rotten to the core,' Slessor said, swayed by Moran's quiet manner. 'I think the captain is right. The fact that Gaines is still in charge of your gambling is giving a wrong impression to the soldiers. And the least you should have done was repay the losses suffered by the soldiers.

91

That would have eased the situation, and the soldiers would probably have kept their hands off your property.'

'Don't throw this business into my lap,' Brannigan said sharply. 'I'm the one who's losing in this, the one who needs protection, and it's gonna cost me at least a thousand bucks to repair the back of the saloon.'

The back door to the saloon slammed with a crash that reverberated, and all heads turned to check on the disturbance. Will Thomas, the town carpenter, who had entered, grinned as he looked around. He was a big man, with powerful arms and a large head. He dropped several lengths of timber on the floor near the office and came across to the bar.

'Do I have to pay for a drink while I'm working for you, Brannigan?' he demanded.

'You can have a beer,' Brannigan said grudgingly, and motioned to Sharkey, the bartender, to fill a glass. 'Working out back, you wouldn't have heard the

news. Pyke was brought in across his saddle some time ago. He was killed ambushing Colonel Denton on the trail from the fort. Denton is dead. How come Pyke wasn't working with you today?'

The carpenter's face lost its smile and turned pale with shock. 'Pyke dead?' he repeated. 'I got word from his wife this morning that he was sick. And he ambushed the colonel? Hell, I though he was just talking when he threatened to kill a soldier.'

'You heard him make a threat against a soldier?' Moran demanded.

'Who are you?' Thomas asked.

'He's a military policeman,' Brannigan said quickly. 'You better be careful how you answer him.'

'I'll settle for the truth,' Moran said. 'What did Pyke say about killing a soldier?'

Thomas picked up the beer that had been placed before him and drank deeply. He set the glass back on the bar and wiped his mouth on his sleeve

before looking at Moran.

'Well?' Moran demanded.

'Pyke always talked big,' Thomas said. 'I never believed the half of what he said. His daughter was attacked by a soldier about a month ago, and he never stopped talking about what he'd do to that soldier if he ever caught up with him. And you say he killed Colonel Denton? Hell, I wouldn't have thought the colonel had anything to do with the attack on Mary Pyke.'

'Pyke was with John Benn,' Moran said. 'They ambushed the colonel when he left the fort to come into town.'

'Have you talked to Benn?' Thomas asked. 'Him and Pyke were thick as thieves.'

'Benn is dead,' Brannigan said.

'The hell you say!' Thomas shook his head. 'I can't believe this. Who killed them?'

'I showed up at the scene when they were attacking the colonel,' Moran said. 'I took a hand, and was forced to kill them both.' He paused, then asked,

'Where does Pyke's wife live?'

'Has she been told about her husband?' Slessor cut in.

'You'll have to ask the sheriff about that.' Moran shrugged.

Slessor left quickly, and his departure broke up the gathering. Other men went out, and Moran considered what he had learned. There was a motive for the killing of Colonel Denton. Pyke wanted to kill the soldier who had assaulted his daughter, but apparently had settled for the first soldier he saw on the day he decided to act. Obviously, Colonel Denton had been in the wrong place at the wrong time. But why had John Benn accompanied Pyke on his grim chore?

Boots thudded on the bare boards of the saloon and Moran glanced to his left to see a tall man dressed in a black broadcloth suit descending the stairs at the far end of the room. The man's face was badly bruised, and Moran glanced at Brannigan.

'The cheating gambler, I presume,'

Moran observed.

'In person,' Brannigan replied with a grimace. 'It's Elroy Gaines.' He raised his voice and called the gambler. 'Come and have a drink, Gaines,' he offered. 'There's someone here who wants to talk to you about the cheating that started all the trouble around here.'

Gaines came forward, a scowl on his injured face. He gazed at Moran with hostility in his dark eyes.

'This is Provost Captain Moran,' Brannigan introduced. 'He's in town to check on the complaints made by the soldiers you cheated.'

Gaines spoke sharply. 'I've never cheated in my life.'

'I have a witness who says he saw you palming cards on more than one occasion,' Moran said.

'Then you'd better bring him to make his accusation to my face,' Gained replied.

'I'll do better than that,' Moran told him smoothly. 'I'll have him in court to give sworn evidence against you if you

are charged with cheating.'

'It'll be my word against his,' Gaines sneered.

'You wouldn't want this witness against you,' Brannigan said with a grin.

Moran turned away and walked to the batwings. He paused and glanced over his shoulder to see Gaines taking a drink from the bartender, and could hear the gambler demanding to know the name of the unknown witness. Moran left the saloon.

Brannigan waited until Moran had gone before leaning towards Will Thomas, the carpenter. 'You'd better drink that beer and then get back to work,' he said. 'I want the job done as fast as you can get it finished.'

Thomas grinned, drained his glass, went back to where he had dropped the timber when he came in, and began to take it into Brannigan's office. Brannigan placed a hand on Gaines's arm.

'What are you gonna do about this situation, Elroy?' he demanded. 'You

can't leave it where it is.'

'What can I do?' Gaines demanded.

'If I were in your boots I'd know what to do.'

'You're a lot smarter than me, so tell me what you'd do.'

'I'd put a slug into that captain's back the first chance I got.'

'You've got to be kidding!' Gaines gazed at Brannigan as if he could not believe his ears. 'Why would I wanta do that?'

'Because he's gonna nail you to the barn door before you're very much older, that's why. Don't be fooled by his quiet manner. He's a sharp killer behind his smooth appearance. Jake Woodson was in here earlier with Del Manning and another of his riders. We were talking business when Moran came in. Woodson's rider, Gann, was a deserter from the army. He recognized Moran from last year and drew on him without warning. Moran killed him from a cold draw. So be warned. And Moran has got Sheriff Steadman as a

witness of your cheating, so don't count on getting the better of them if you go to trial.'

'They can't prove anything against me.' Gaines shrugged. 'I know the odds. It's my word against all comers. They got no proof. And who's talking about a trial?'

'The game is going against you,' Brannigan said. 'If you wanta stay on here then you'll do like I said. Kill Moran the first chance you get.'

'Are you planning to fire me?'

'It looks like I might have to. Slessor thinks it will defuse the trouble if you go. I want to keep you on, but not while Moran is hanging around. Pyke did a stupid thing, going out like he did and killing the colonel. I paid him to shoot a soldier in the back in a dark alley, not pick on the commanding officer of the fort. What the hell got into him?'

'You can't trust anyone these days.' Gaines turned away from the bar. 'OK, I'll take care of that captain when it gets dark.'

'Make sure you do a good job,' Brannigan warned. 'You'll only get one chance, and if you handle it wrong you'll be dead.'

* * *

Moran walked along the sidewalk to the law office, his thoughts racing as he considered the situation. He saw a tall, lean man in a black town suit; his pale face was wearing a dolorous expression, and he was leading the horses carrying the bodies of Benn and Pyke along the street away from the jail. They were followed by several townsmen who had nothing better to do than waste time. Sheriff Steadman was standing in the doorway of the office, his expression grim. He straightened when he saw Moran, then turned and went into the office when Moran reached him.

'There's not much you can do about the colonel's death,' Steadman said when Moran joined him in the office. 'You killed the ambushers, which is a

pity. You might have learned something from them. Now we might never know what was going on in Pyke's mind.'

'I heard in the saloon that Pyke's daughter was assaulted by a soldier, and Pyke had talked to the town carpenter about doing something about it. I'll go along and talk to Pyke's widow shortly. She might be able to tell me something of Pyke's attitude of late. Where does she live?'

'There's a side street just past the bank with two rows of houses. Pyke lived in the last house in the right-hand row.'

'I'll go along there now and get it over with,' Moran said.

'I'm riding out of town,' Steadman said. 'I need to check up on my deputy.'

They left the office together. Steadman mounted his horse, which was standing at the hitch rail, and rode away along the street. Moran walked along the sidewalk to the right, passed the bank and turned into the side street. He went to the last house on the right and

paused at the gate to admire the flower garden. The town mayor, Byron Slessor, was emerging from the house, hat in hand, and a tall, attractive woman appeared behind him, her face grey with shock.

Moran opened the gate and, as he moved into the garden, a rifle hammered sharply somewhere to his right. He heard the crackle of a bullet passing his left ear and threw himself down into a flower-bed.

5

Moran hit the dirt, then got to his feet swiftly, palming his gun as he did so. The echoes of the shot were growling away across the town. He saw Slessor urging Mrs Pyke back into the house, following her and closing the door. He turned in the direction from which the shot had come and saw a rider on a grey horse galloping fast towards him along the side street, with a rifle in his right hand. When Moran reached full height the rider levelled his rifle one-handed and fired another shot. Moran ducked, and the slug passed through the spot his head would have occupied had he not moved. He stayed bent double and moved to his right a couple of yards.

The sound of approaching hoofs was urgent as he straightened again. The rider was leaning forward in his saddle

to minimize his target area, and snapped off another shot when he saw Moran, who ducked yet again. He went back to his left, and when he straightened again the rider had gone by and was swinging right to get behind the cover of the house. Moran fired two quick, hastily aimed shots, and muttered a curse when the rider disappeared out of sight along the side of the house with the slugs crackling past him.

Moran jumped over the white-painted picket fence, gun ready, but the rider had already passed around the corner to the back of the house. He ran fast in pursuit, turned the corner and lifted his gun again, only to see the rider turning left into the main street and vanishing quickly from sight. He heaved a sigh, halted and reloaded his spent chambers. His face was grim as he went back to the front garden, where Slessor was emerging from the house, his fleshy face pale and filled with apprehension.

'Who was that?' Slessor demanded when Moran stood before him.

'I have no idea, but I'll know his horse again if I see it,' Moran replied. He looked past the town mayor; saw Mrs Pyke standing in her doorway. He asked: 'How did she take the news of her husband's death?'

'Not well at all,' Slessor sighed. 'Do you have to talk to her right now? She's badly shocked.'

'There's no such thing as a good time to talk to a woman about the death of her husband.' Moran stepped around Slessor and went to the door of the house.

Mrs Pyke's face was tear-streaked. She was a tall, slender woman around forty.

'Mr Slessor has told me who you are,' she said in a trembling tone. 'You'd better come in.'

Moran entered the house and she closed the door on Slessor, who had made as if to enter. She led the way into the parlour and invited Moran to sit

down. He chose a straight-backed chair near the window overlooking the garden, and glanced out to see Slessor leaving.

'I am sorry to intrude at a time like this,' said Moran gently. 'I'm wondering if you can tell me something of your husband's demeanour this morning before he left you. It is most important that I learn everything I can about him.'

'You're a military policeman, aren't you? You killed my husband.'

'That's true. I left the fort this morning about half an hour behind Colonel Denton, heard shooting on the trail, and found the colonel under fire. He was being bush-whacked. I went to his aid, and in the shooting that followed your husband and a man called John Benn were killed.'

'I knew Adam had something on his mind,' said Mrs Pyke tremulously. 'I heard him threaten to find and kill the soldier who had attacked our daughter, but I didn't think he would go so far as to shoot the colonel.'

'Can you throw any light on John Benn being in your husband's company? Benn works for Brannigan at the saloon, I believe.'

'I have no idea why they were together. John Benn is not the kind of man my husband would associate with. That they were together this morning came as a complete surprise to me, and for them to go out and murder an innocent soldier is beyond my understanding.'

'Is your daughter at home?' Moran asked. 'I'd like to ask her for details of the assault she suffered. I'll endeavour to find the soldier who was responsible and see that he is punished for what he did.'

'She is not here. She moved to my sister's home in Denver after the attack, and nothing will induce her to return.'

'Your husband was working on the damage in the saloon caused by the fire, wasn't he? But he took the day off to go out and kill a soldier. Did you have any intimation of what was in his mind?'

'Not in so many words. All he said to me before he left the house was that he had been paid to do a special job, and I assumed that was the repair work at the saloon.'

'Do you have any idea who paid him?'

Mrs Pyke shook her head.

'Or what the job was?' Moran pressed.

'Adam didn't say.'

Moran nodded and prepared to leave, aware that he would make no further progress. He left the grieving widow and heaved a sigh of relief as he walked back to the main street. He went to the livery barn and sought out Otis Jary. The livery man was seated at the desk in his small office, eating a sandwich. A whiskey bottle and a half-empty glass stood at his right elbow.

'I heard some shooting a short while ago,' Jary said.

'A man riding a grey horse fired some shots at me,' Moran admitted.

'He was a medium-sized man wearing a blue shirt. I got a look at the horse. It was grey with a dark patch on its left rump.'

'There are several grey horses around town,' Jary mused, 'and most of them have dark patches. Nothing comes to mind, likewise the rider in a blue shirt. Maybe he didn't leave his horse here in the barn.'

'It was just a long shot,' Moran said. 'Keep your eyes open, will you?'

'Sure. I'll do anything for law and order.'

Moran went for his horse hitched outside the law office and paused for a moment to look around the street. His gaze rested on the entrance to the hotel, and Mrs Rogers, the murdered sutler's widow, came to mind. He left his horse and walked to the hotel. Slessor was standing at the reception desk, chatting to a middle-aged lady who was seated behind it. Slessor turned at the sound of Moran's boots on the pine floor, and came forward, forcing a smile.

'Did you have any luck with Mrs Pyke?' Slessor asked.

Moran shook his head. 'I didn't expect her to know anything,' he replied. 'I'd like to see Mrs Rogers now.'

Slessor heaved a sigh and shook his head. 'That poor woman,' he said. 'It isn't enough that she's lost her husband. She has to be hounded and questioned to distraction. It would be a kindness if you could leave her alone.'

'I can't do that.' Moran shook his head. 'I'm investigating her husband's murder, and she is an important witness to his last hours. What she may have to say will probably be more important than the testimony of all other witnesses.'

'I've talked to her, and from what she says I believe she knows nothing that would help your inquiry.'

'What room is she in?' Moran said bluntly, cutting through Slessor's droning voice.

'Up the stairs, and it's the second

door on the right. I'll show you up.'

'Thanks, but I can find my own way.'

Slessor frowned and moved away. Moran went to the stairs and ascended. As he reached the top a woman approached from along the corridor to the right. She paused to wait until he cleared the stairs, and he stopped, barring her way. 'Excuse me, but are you Mrs Rogers?' he challenged.

'I am.' Her voice was low, filled with barely suppressed emotion. She was tall and slender, aged around forty; an attractive woman with high cheekbones and dark eyes. 'Who are you?' she demanded.

'I'm Provost Captain Slade Moran, ma'am. I arrived at the fort this morning to investigate your husband's murder, and I need to talk to you.'

'I told the inquiry at the fort everything I knew, which was next to nothing. Unfortunately, Tom didn't confide in me at all. I was not aware of anything he did in business or in his private life.'

'I have read the statement you made at the inquiry,' Moran said, 'and I gained the impression that you held back on some aspects of your husband's life.'

'You think I was lying?' she demanded, and a slow stain of colour seeped into her pale cheeks. Her tone hardened. 'I resent the implication, Captain.'

'I'm not hinting at anything,' he replied. 'But you were closer to your husband than anyone at the fort. He must have talked to you about his business and made remarks on some of the soldiers he mingled with. I need to learn something of the background of his life, and you're the only person likely to have that knowledge. You want your husband's killer to be caught, don't you?'

'Naturally. But it is well known that a soldier named Green killed him.'

'I arrested Green a week ago and brought him back to the fort. He told me he did not kill your husband.'

'And you believed him?'

'I don't take any evidence at face value.' Moran shook his head. 'I do not accept anything I am told in the course of an investigation unless I can prove it to my satisfaction. I listen to what I'm told, but I also watch the people I question, and through experience I can usually sense when someone is either lying or holding something back.'

'I'm not holding anything back,' she said strongly, and for a moment her dark eyes became animated. 'I don't wish to talk about my private life, but I will tell you that my husband and I did not have a normal relationship. He went his own way, and did not include me in anything he did. Beyond that I have nothing more to say, and I hope you will respect my wishes.'

'I have no desire to probe beyond questions which will give me an idea of your husband's last days. For instance, did he mention having trouble with any soldiers in the course of his business? Was he afraid of any one?'

'He never confided in me about anything to do with his business. He went his own sweet way without reference to me, and I stayed in the background, making a life for myself without him as best I could.'

'You must have led a most boring life,' Moran suggested.

The faintest hint of a smile touched her pale lips but was gone in a flash. Her eyes seemed to lose what little expression they contained, and she sighed and shook her head.

'There were many times when I wanted to run as far as I could from my husband, but I stayed with him.'

Moran nodded. 'What are your plans now?' he asked.

She shrugged and shook her head. 'I don't have any at the moment. My husband is dead and I don't have a future. I'd like to leave it at that.'

'I may have to talk to you again,' he warned.

'I'm sure you'll find me if you do,' she countered.

Moran touched the brim of his hat and turned to descend the stairs. He left the hotel, returned to his horse, and swung into the saddle. Aware that he was wasting time in town, he rode out and headed back to the fort.

* * *

Jake Woodson jogged along the trail out of town, waiting for Del Manning to catch up with him. When they left town Manning had reined in and turned his horse around.

'There's something I gotta do, Jake. You go on and I'll catch up with you. I won't be more than fifteen minutes.'

'If you're gonna do what I think you're gonna do then watch your step. The guy who killed Gann will be no pushover.'

Manning grinned. 'My name's not Gann,' he responded, and galloped back into town.

Woodson continued at a canter, his thoughts sombre. He had liked Gann,

115

and had not known the man was a deserter. He had been shocked when Gann drew his gun without warning, and even more shocked when Moran had beaten Gann to the draw. He continued steadily until the sound of hoofs echoed on his back trail, and when he looked back over his shoulder he saw Manning galloping to catch up.

'We better put some distance between us and town, Jake,' Manning declared. 'I made a hash of shooting Moran.'

'If he follows us out of town we'll bury him where he won't be found,' Woodson replied. Nevertheless he increased his pace, and turned off the trail to ride across country.

'So what did Brannigan have to talk about in the saloon?' Manning demanded when they dismounted on a ridge an hour later to give their horses a breather.

'He's got a special job for us.' Woodson's keen eyes crinkled as he gazed across wild countryside at the

distant mountains.

'We're working with him now on this horse-stealing business,' Manning observed.

'This is a one-off job.' Woodson laughed. 'And you'll never guess what it is in a million years.'

'I ain't into guessing,' said Manning sourly. 'So what is it?'

'The banker in Lodgepole wants someone to rob his bank. Brannigan gave me all the details, and we're gonna do the job Friday around noon. We don't even have to rob the bank. We go through the motions and the dough will be handed to us. We hit the banker over the head and walk out. The banker will raise the alarm when we've got clear.'

'You gotta be joking!' Manning gazed at Woodson in disbelief. When he got no reaction he asked: 'So what's in it for the banker?'

'We take a handful of dough for doing the job, and give the rest of it to Brannigan, who returns it to the

banker; who also gets insurance for his losses.'

'Can you beat that? A crooked banker! Do you trust Brannigan?'

'With my life,' Woodson replied.

'That's what it will cost you if anything goes wrong,' Manning rasped.

'I've worked with Brannigan before. He's back of this horse-deal we're working on. He told me the banker has a share in the saloon, and needs dough to keep his head above water.'

'A man shouldn't oughta jump in the creek if he can't swim,' Manning observed. 'What are they gonna pay for us to walk in there and take the bank's money?'

'It'll be a thousand dollars.'

'And how much do we lift from the bank?' Manning persisted.

'About twenty thousand bucks!'

'So what's to stop us riding on with all the bank money when we've get our paws on it? We wouldn't need to do all that hard work stealing horses and selling them on to the army.'

'I've already thought of that!' Woodson grinned. 'But we'll string along for a spell.'

'One of these days you'll come unstuck with your underhand dealing.'

'I reckon we can pick up a helluva lot more than just the money from the bank — if we play our cards right.'

'What about the trouble in Lodgepole between the army and the town? That could give us problems.' Manning studied their back trail, looking for signs of pursuit.

'Brannigan is stoking up that trouble for his own ends. Don't ask me what it's all about because I don't know. He wouldn't talk about it, but you can bet he's on to a good thing, and we'll get a big share of whatever it is.'

'It'll need to be good. We're getting in pretty deep now. I reckon that sheriff looked twice at us in the saloon when Gann was killed. And he reckons to come out to the creek and give us the once-over.'

Woodson nodded. 'If he comes

sniffing around we'll bury him. Brannigan wants him out of the way anyhow.
Now stop asking damn fool questions
and let's get on. The colonel at the fort
is dead, and Brannigan wanted him
removed because he was too damn
honest. Brannigan reckons a Major
Hopwood is in line to take over
command at the fort now Denton's
gone, and he's in Brannigan's back
pocket.'

'So Brannigan paid Pyke to kill the
colonel.' Manning laughed. 'That's
what I call playing cards close to your
vest.'

They mounted and rode on. Manning was thinking that the whole
scheme was getting too complicated for
his liking, but he trusted Woodson to
keep them on top of whatever happened.

The range grew wilder as they
continued, and when they reached a
ridge where they could look down on
the spread they had taken over,
Manning jerked his horse back off the

crest and hissed a warning to Woodson.

'Get back out of sight, Jake. I caught a flash of sunlight on glass,'

Woodson turned his horse instantly and rode back off the skyline.

'Where did you see it?' he demanded.

'Just beneath the yellow rock that's overhanging the shack. It looks like someone is spying on us with long-distance glasses. Stay here and I'll work my way around the rock and come up on him from the far side.'

'OK, I'll go on and ride into the ranch to keep him occupied. When you get him, bring him down to the shack.'

Woodson rode over the ridge and headed on down the long slope to level ground. Manning rode to the left and angled along the ridge just below the skyline until he was beyond the yellow rock. He dismounted and left his horse on a rocky ledge, trailed his reins, and checked his gun. He dropped to the ground and crawled forward until he could look down on the yellow rock. He saw a man lying full length on the

ground in the cover of the rock, and twenty yards back a horse was standing with trailing reins. Manning saw the man using a pair of field glasses. In the background, Woodson was riding down to the spread, apparently unaware that he had company, and the watching man was following Woodson's progress through his glasses.

Manning sneaked towards the rock, moving slowly and carefully, his pistol in his right hand, cocked and ready for action. He got within five yards of the yellow rock before the watching man heard him and swung around, his right hand moving quickly to his holstered gun.

'Don't try it,' Manning called. 'Stand up, and keep your hands clear of your waist.'

The man arose and lifted his hands shoulder high. He was tall and lean, around twenty-five years old, fresh-faced. A law star was pinned to his shirt front, glinting in the evening sunlight as he gazed at Manning.

'Who are you, mister?' the deputy demanded.

'I'm Del Manning. I work on that hoss ranch you're watching, and I wanta know what you're doing up here, spying on the place.'

'I'm Dick Mossley, from Lodgepole. I was over to Rafter O last night, checking out a complaint that they'd lost twenty horses to thieves. When Chuck Osman mentioned that one of his riders rode by here a couple of days ago and saw an outfit working the place I came over for a looksee. And whaddya know? The first thing I did when I got here was recognize a hoss down there that was stolen from Rafter O some days ago.'

'You recognized a horse?' Manning grinned. 'That sure takes some believing.'

'No doubt about it,' Mossley said. 'It belongs to Tilda Osman, Chuck's daughter. Tilda is my gal. She's had that chestnut since it was born, and I could pick it out from among a

thousand horses.'

'So what are you gonna do about it?' Manning demanded.

'I'm gonna ride to town, get a posse, and come on back here to grab Osman's hosses back.'

Manning shook his head. 'You ain't,' he said. 'Shuck your guns, and then you and me are gonna ride down to the spread and you can talk to Jake Woodson, who runs the outfit. Your long nose has got you into a load of trouble, Deputy. Get your horse and head for the spread down there. Don't try to get smart. Any fool play will get you killed.'

Mossley disarmed himself, went to his horse and gathered the reins. He led the animal to the left and followed the line of the ridge. Manning collected his horse on the way and swung into the saddle. Mossley jumped into his saddle and they continued down to the ranch.

Woodson was standing in front of the shack when they rode in. He gazed at the law badge on Mossley's chest as if

he had never seen one before.

'We got ourselves a real curly wolf of a lawman here,' Manning observed.

'Is that a fact?' Woodson shook his head. 'Get rid of him.'

'We'd better think some more about this,' Manning went on. 'The next thing we know, that pesky sheriff in Lodgepole will be riding in here with a big posse. This was supposed to be a slick job, but it seems the whole county is wise to us and what we're gonna do. I don't like any part of it, and the sooner we ride out the better off we'll be.'

'Are you getting nervous?' Woodson demanded. 'I never thought I'd see the day. Tell me who else knows about our deal?' He paused for Manning's answer, but all he got was a shrug of the shoulders. 'Then I'll tell you. This long-nose deputy is the only one, and he's way out on a limb. We cut him down and no one's the wiser. Take him round the back and put a bullet through him. If the sheriff calls we'll bury him beside this galoot.'

Manning waved his gun. 'You heard the man. Ride around the shack and get off your hoss.'

Mossley's face had turned pale, and for a moment he looked as if he would refuse to move. Manning cocked his pistol and levelled it at the deputy's chest. Mossley heaved a sigh and touched spurs to the flanks of his horse. He guided the animal around the shack, reined in, and sat his saddle, looking into Manning's face. Manning was grinning. He squeezed his trigger and the crash of the shot blasted through the heavy silence, sending a wave of echoes across the desolate country.

The bullet struck Mossley in the centre of the chest and he went over backwards, arms flying wide. His horse bucked in fright. Mossley fell out of the saddle and thumped on the hard ground. The horse ran to the corral and halted there. Manning dismounted, checked Mossley, satisfying himself that he was dead, then led his

horse across to the corral. He unsaddled both horses and turned them into the corral, then stood for a moment watching the chestnut that Mossley had said belonged to Tilda Osman. Gun echoes still rolled and grumbled in the distance as he walked back around the shack.

Woodson was waiting for him in the doorway.

'You'll have to bury him now,' he said, and Manning grimaced. 'And I've changed my mind,' he continued. 'I didn't like the look the sheriff gave me back in Brannigan's place. I think he guessed right off that we're the horse-thieves, so I'm gonna play it safe. We're pulling out until after we hit that bank on Friday. I'll take the rest of the gang and those horses in the corrals up to the mountain meadow where we were staying until Brannigan sent for me. The horses will go on from there to a fort further north. You'll stay here, Del.'

'The hell you say!' Manning cut in.

His grin faded. 'I ain't sticking around here. That sheriff might turn up with a posse, and that could mean a lot of trouble.'

'Shut up and listen to me. Brannigan wants the sheriff dead, and you won't get a better chance if he comes out here, which I expect him to do. If he shows up with a posse, shoot him from a distance and then hit your saddle and come up to the mountain meadow. If he rides in alone, kill him, bury him beside his deputy, and then make your way to Lodgepole. Report to Brannigan, tell him what you've done, and stay in town until I show up for the bank job on Friday.'

Manning considered for a moment and then nodded.

'Sounds OK,' he mused. 'I'll do it. I reckon we'd be stupid to stick around now, anyway, and the sooner you get moving the better.'

'I'll wait for the gang to get back,' Woodson said. 'They should bring in another dozen horses. We'll be long

gone before anyone from town shows up. Give that sheriff time to get out here is all I ask.'

'He's as good as dead,' replied Manning with a grin.

6

Moran caught up with an army wagon that was returning to the fort after picking up Colonel Denton's body. A squad of six troopers under the command of Lieutenant Wiley surrounded the wagon. Wiley saluted Moran. The fort showed in the distance, stark in the late afternoon sunshine. Lieutenant Wiley's rugged face was lined with shock as he gazed at Moran.

'I understand you were at the scene of the ambush and dealt with the two ambushers, Captain,' Wiley said with a quiver of emotion in his tone. 'Is it true you killed both?'

Moran rode in beside the lieutenant and gave an account of what had occurred. Wiley shook his head.

'I don't understand how those ambushers knew the colonel was riding

130

to town at that time,' he mused.

'I'm wondering about that myself,' Moran admitted. 'But I learned in town that one of the killers may have set out this morning with the intention of shooting a soldier, and just happened to meet the colonel. It looks as if the colonel was in the wrong place at the wrong time. What I'd like to know is why the colonel was riding into town unescorted.'

'I think it had to do with the trouble in the town between soldiers and the men running the saloon there.' Wiley shook his head. 'And I think there will be a lot more trouble when the men learn about this. Colonel Denton was well liked. Major Hopwood is second in command at the fort. He may take over command, and he's not popular.'

Moran was thoughtful as they continued, and when they reached the fort he rode to the company office and dismounted. Top Sergeant Grimmer was standing in the doorway of the office, bareheaded and grim-faced, his

gaze on the wagon as it crossed the parade ground. A squad of men at drill on the square were brought to attention as the wagon passed them. The escort was dismissed and rode off to the horse lines. Grimmer saluted Moran, and asked the inevitable question. Moran explained the action that had taken place at the ambush site, and Grimmer nodded approvingly when he heard that the two ambushers had been killed.

'Sergeant Grove rode in with the news, Captain,' Grimmer said. 'Major Hopwood's first reaction was to take some men into town and raise hell. But he calmed down eventually.'

Moran frowned, not liking the thought of angry soldiers with mayhem in mind descending on a peaceful community.

'It's a pity you were forced to kill both ambushers, sir,' Grimmer continued. 'Now we'll never know what happened at the scene of the ambush. The colonel hardly ever left the fort, and those two killers were out there

waiting for him.'

'I think they were out looking for any soldier, and the colonel was unfortunate to run into them. One of the killers was a man called Pyke. It seems his daughter was assaulted in town by a soldier some time ago, and Pyke wanted revenge. Was the case reported here?'

'Yes, sir, it was. The sheriff came out and there was a big inquiry, but the guilty soldier was not apprehended. The girl in question was brought to the fort and there was an identity parade, but she couldn't pick out the man who attacked her so nothing could be done about the assault. I think that was the start of the trouble, Captain. Everything seemed to happen from that time.'

Moran entered the office and Grimmer followed him closely.

'The other matter giving me a problem is the suicide of Trooper Green,' Moran said. 'I had Green under arrest for over a week, and got to know him pretty well on our return here. I

didn't get the impression he was the type to end his own life. He swore that he did not kill the sutler, and said he would be able to prove his innocence. So what kind of a man was he?'

'He had a drink problem, Captain; otherwise he was a good soldier,' Grimmer said. 'It seems that Rogers was killed after he refused to give Green a bottle of whiskey on credit. You've seen the report of the incident, and it was fairly obvious that Green was involved.'

'It was not an open and shut case against Green,' Moran mused. 'I'll question everyone who gave evidence at the inquiry, but I'm more interested at this time in why Green ended up hanged in his cell. The big question is: how did he get hold of the cord he used? Sergeant Buller appears to be an efficient soldier. Apparently he carried out his job to the letter of military law, as did the rest of the provost section, and yet Green hanged himself with a piece of rope that was not in his

possession when he was placed in the cell.'

'I'm sure Sergeant Buller will come up with the answer to that one, Captain,' Grimmer said confidently. 'He runs the police section with a rod of iron and doesn't deviate from the book. I had a talk with him, and he understands the implications of the situation.'

'Such as?' Moran asked.

'He knows he'll carry the can for what happened if he doesn't get at the truth. He's a top-class man at his job, and takes it personally if anything goes wrong. You'd better see Major Hopwood now, sir. He's taken over here pending orders from headquarters. He's in the colonel's office.'

'Show me in,' Moran said.

Grimmer tapped at the door of the inner office, opened it, and addressed the major. Then he turned and motioned for Moran to enter.

'The major will see you now, sir.'

Moran entered the office. Major

Hopwood arose from the desk and came around it with outstretched hand. He was tall and lean, bronzed by the sun, quite handsome, and looked to be in his middle forties. He wore a thick black moustache which enhanced his general appearance. His uniform fitted him as if he had been poured into it.

'I'm pleased to meet you, Captain,' he greeted. 'I was told you had arrived and brought Trooper Green back with you. I understand you'll be staying here to look into our local trouble. It was a stroke of luck you got to the colonel in time to kill his attackers.'

'I think the trouble in town will fizzle out,' Moran said. 'I'm more concerned at the moment about Green's suicide.'

'Green was a deserter and probably a murderer,' Hopwood said. 'I'm not going to waste any sympathy on him.'

'I have to get the facts of what happened,' Moran said.

'I'm sure you'll do a good job. Let me know if I can help in any way. If

there's anything you need then just speak up and it will be yours. All I ask is that you keep me informed of your progress.'

'I'll certainly do that, Major,' Moran replied. He saluted and left the office.

Sergeant Buller emerged from the guardhouse as Moran reached the outer door, and he saluted smartly.

'I want to talk to you and your staff again, Sergeant,' Moran said. 'Have you discovered yet how the cord Green hanged himself with came to be in his cell?'

'No, sir.' Buller stood rigidly to attention, his face expressionless. 'Corporal Bessey is the man on the spot about that, Captain. He was in charge of the guardhouse at the time.'

'Is he still here? If he isn't then fetch him, and I'll want Johnson as well. I'll wait inside.'

Buller saluted and departed. Moran entered the guardhouse and a trooper seated at the desk sprang to his feet and saluted.

'I'm Provost Captain Moran. Who are you?'

'Trooper Devlin, sir.'

'At ease, Devlin. I'll sit behind the desk. You pull up a chair opposite. I want to talk about the murder of the sutler. Where were you at the time Rogers was killed?'

'I was in the trading post that night, Captain, in the company of Trooper Green. We used to go around together. I liked Green.'

'I didn't see your name in the file from the inquiry. Didn't you come forward and report your presence that evening?'

'I didn't, sir, because I thought it wouldn't help the inquiry.'

'So tell me what happened on that evening.'

'Green was confined to the post for being involved in the trouble in Lodgepole. He wasn't supposed to be in the trading post at all.'

'Was he one of the men who attacked the gambler caught cheating in the saloon?'

'He incited the attack, after catching the gambler cheating.'

'The men who beat up the gambler are under open arrest,' Moran mused. 'If Green was one of them then, as you pointed out, he shouldn't have been in the trading post.'

'It was widely known around the fort that the trouble was down to Green, and everyone agreed that what he did was right.'

'So what were the events on the evening of the murder?'

'Green was drinking in the trading post. He had a drink problem, and was always bending the rules. He'd lost money to the gambler in the saloon and was broke, so he asked the sutler for a bottle of whiskey on the slate. Rogers refused and, after an argument, Green left. He must have returned later and confronted Rogers again.'

'Did anyone actually see Green stab Rogers?' Moran asked.

'Not to my knowledge, Captain. If anyone witnessed the attack the odds

were against it being reported.'

'Why was that? Is murder condoned at this fort?'

'No, sir.' Devlin shook his head emphatically. 'Rogers was not liked generally. He was a nasty type, unfriendly and aggressive, especially when he had been drinking. Sometimes he beat his wife, but no one would put the finger on him, although Green did confront him about it. So when Rogers was killed, no one stood up for him.'

'Was Green interested in Mrs Rogers?'

Devlin suppressed a sigh and remained silent.

'Well?' Moran demanded. 'Answer my question.'

'Now Green is dead it won't hurt him if I tell you what I know. Mrs Rogers was a lonely woman and Green used to meet her in Lodgepole. They had something going for months, until Rogers got suspicious and began to watch his wife's movements.'

'Did Rogers catch them together?'

'I can't say. All I know is that Green

had it in for Rogers, and if he killed Rogers then it wasn't over a bottle of whiskey.'

'I'll want a statement from you about what you've just told me. It gives a whole new slant on the murder. Does anyone else know about this?'

'Not to my knowledge, sir. Green told me about his doings because he knew it wouldn't go any further. As to making a statement, Captain, I will if nobody else gets to read it. There are other men at the fort with an interest in Mrs Rogers.'

'Is that a fact? Name them.'

'I can but I won't, sir. It would be more than my life is worth.'

'Very well, we'll leave it there for the moment. I'll get a statement from you later. Thanks for what you've told me.'

The door was opened at that moment and Sergeant Buller entered, followed by Corporal Bessey and Trooper Johnson. Devlin got to his feet immediately, saluted and departed quickly.

'Corporal Bessey,' Moran said. 'Sit down.' He waited until Bessey was seated, and then looked at Buller: 'That will be all, Sergeant. These interviews will be private. You and Johnson can leave us alone. Go into the cells or step outside on to the porch — anywhere out of earshot. I'll let you know when I get through.'

Sergeant Buller opened his mouth as if to protest but thought better of it and turned away, motioning for Johnson to accompany him. They went out to the porch. Moran gazed at Corporal Bessey for several moments before speaking. The corporal was looking uneasy, his forehead beaded with sweat.

'So what really happened when Green was brought in this morning?' Moran said at length.

'I've told you, sir.' Bessey's tone sounded impatient. 'There's nothing I can add to what I said before.'

'You cannot account for the cord Green used to hang himself?'

'That's right, Captain.'

142

'Well, it's not good enough. You were responsible for Green's welfare, and they'll throw the book at you if you can't answer the simple question: how did the cord get into Green's possession?'

'It's beyond me, sir. I don't know the answer.'

'Of course you know.' Moran's tone roughened. 'I brought Green to the fort this morning, and he certainly didn't have the cord on him when I handed him over. You searched him thoroughly before locking him in the cell, and no one else went near him except you, Johnson, and Sergeant Buller. So what happened?'

'I can vouch for Johnson and myself, sir. Green didn't get the cord from either of us.'

'You're implying that Sergeant Buller must have passed the cord to Green.'

'No, sir. I'm not making an accusation. That's how it comes out. If Johnson and I didn't do it then it leaves Sergeant Buller on the spot.'

'I shall be talking to Sergeant Buller in a moment,' said Moran impatiently.

He regarded Bessey analytically, his thoughts going over the situation. It did not seem feasible that someone would pass the cord to Green, and if that was what happened it did not follow that Green would hang himself with it. Moran thought back to the week he and Green had spent together returning to the fort, and he knew that suicide had been the last thing on Green's mind. But Green might have given up hope the moment he was locked in the cell. And if the rope had not been given to him then what was the alternative? Moran sighed and motioned to Bessey.

'That will be all for now, Corporal. Tell Sergeant Buller to come in.'

Bessey was relieved and left hurriedly. A moment later Sergeant Buller entered and Moran pointed to the seat in front of the desk.

'Sit down, Sergeant.' He waited until had Buller had complied. 'I think it is ridiculous to suppose that someone

handed Green the cord, don't you?'

'Yes, sir, I do,' Buller said instantly.

'So what do you think happened?'

A frown appeared on Buller's heavy features. He thought for a moment before shaking his head. 'I have no idea, Captain.'

'It's quite simple really.' Moran spoke softly. 'Green didn't have the cord on him and the three men guarding him did not give it to him, so what is the only other option?'

'I'm sure I don't know, Captain.'

'I do.' A faint smiled showed briefly on Moran's lips. 'Someone took the cord into the cell but didn't give it to Green — who probably wouldn't have wanted to commit suicide anyway — and that someone put the cord around Green's neck and hanged him from the window bar.'

'Are you serious, Captain?' demanded Buller, a hoarse note sounding in his rasping tone. He leaned forward and gazed intently into Moran's face.

'I'm not saying that is what happened, merely pointing out the alternatives. Which do you think applies, Sergeant? Did someone give that cord to Green because Green asked for it or did someone murder Green by using the cord as I suggested? That's an interesting problem, don't you think? Why would someone want to kill Green?'

'So, if Green didn't hang himself then either Bessey or Johnson murdered him.'

'You haven't included yourself in that possibility, Sergeant.'

'No, sir, because I know I didn't do any such thing.'

'So Bessey and Johnson handled it — is that what you think?'

'You're putting words in my mouth, Captain.' Buller scowled.

Moran shook his head. 'I'm not. I'm looking at a situation and working out what could have happened. I'll question you and the other two to see what you can come up with and go on from

there. You say you didn't murder Green so it stands to reason that one of the other two did.'

'Or both of them,' Buller insisted. He shook his head. 'You're going too deep for me, sir.'

Moran changed the subject abruptly. 'As the police sergeant here, you get to know a lot of things that ordinary soldiers don't pick up. Personally, I don't think that if Green killed Rogers he did it over a bottle of whiskey. There has to be more to it than that. I've learned that Rogers and his wife did not enjoy a normal relationship. So was Mrs Rogers seeing another man?'

'I heard rumours to that effect.' Buller shrugged. 'But as it was none of my business I didn't look into it.'

'Was she seeing a soldier? Green, for instance.'

'Is that what you heard, sir?'

'Just answer the question.'

'I believe she was seeing one of the soldiers here, sir.'

'And it was Green, wasn't it?'

'Yes, sir.'

'That will be all, Sergeant. I'll talk to you again later.'

Moran got to his feet and departed, leaving Buller to gaze after him. He went to the office and told Top Sergeant Grimmer he was going back to town, then fetched his horse and left the fort.

★ ★ ★

Sheriff Steadman rode out of Lodgepole at a canter and headed for the Rafter O ranch. He followed the trail north, and two hours later reined in on a ridge to peer down at the huddle of buildings on level ground at the bottom of the slope. The big corral was empty, and he frowned as he went on. There hadn't been much in the way of horse-stealing for a long time, and he meant to stamp it out before it could spread. When he rode into the yard he found Chuck Osman, the rancher, standing by the corral, shaking his head. Osman, a tall, thin, beanpole of a

man, turned at the sound of hoofs, and heaved a sigh when Steadman swung out of his saddle. His brown eyes were unblinking as he gazed at the stern-faced lawman.

'Twenty horses disappeared as if they sprouted wings and flew over the mountains,' Osman said. 'Even Tilda's horse has gone, and she's heartbroken. She had that horse from the day it was born.'

'I'll get them back if they're still around,' Steadman said. 'Have you seen Mossley out this way?'

'Sure. He was here. I told him I'd got a report that an outfit had moved into that derelict place on Owl Creek and Mossley said he'd ride over that way to look around. I thought he would have come back this way but he hasn't showed.'

'He didn't come back to town either,' Steadman said. 'I got worried about him, so here I am.'

'He's a good man, and can look after himself,' Osman mused. 'Do you think

something bad has happened to him?'

'I hope not. So you didn't see anyone when the horses were taken.' Steadman stepped up into his saddle, gathered his reins, and paused to look down at Osman.

'Not a doggone thing. Sue and me had ridden out to the south that day, and were gone about four hours. When we got back the hosses were missing. I reckon whoever took them must have been watching the spread and didn't want to be seen. I guess we were lucky they didn't ride in and shoot us in cold blood.'

'I'll take a look around Owl Creek,' Steadman said. 'I'll come back this way and let you know what I find. I saw three men in town earlier who said they'd set up on the creek at the old Manson place. I can't say I liked the look of them. One turned out to be an army deserter, and was shot dead by an army troubleshooter who had shown up.'

'You should have brought out a

posse,' Osman said.

'There'll be time for that when I know what's going on,' Steadman replied.

'I found some tracks to the north, but they petered out on hard ground. I reckon my broncs are heading for an army post right now.' Osman lifted a hand in farewell as Steadman rode out.

Shadows were creeping in around Steadman when he reached high ground overlooking Owl Creek. He remained off the skyline and studied the dilapidated spread for a long time. He could see that some work had been done around the place — corrals mended, the big shack fixed up a little. But the place still looked deserted. There were no horses in either corral, and he wondered where Woodson and his crew were — perhaps out raiding another spread in the area. He had a hunch that Woodson was behind the horse-stealing, and looked forward to getting the deadwood on the gang.

He dismounted and sat on a rock to

await full dark. When he could no longer make out features of his surroundings he left his horse knee-hobbled, took his rifle, and set off through the shadows for a closer look at the deserted horse ranch.

Silence enveloped him like a blanket. Stars began to appear overhead, and a faint breeze blew into his face. He slowed when he neared the shack, then halted and stood listening intently. There were no unnatural noises, and no lights anywhere. He wondered about that. He had heard Woodson tell Del Manning they were heading back to this place, so where were they?

He got down on all fours and eased closer to the door of the shack. His eyes were accustomed to the gloom, and he soon realized that the place was deserted. He moved back and returned to his horse and made camp. He had come prepared to stay out through the night, and made a sparse meal of cold food after feeding his horse from a bag of oats tied behind the cantle. Then he

unrolled his bedroll, settled down, and was asleep within minutes.

He did not awaken again. While he slept, Del Manning emerged from the shadows behind the shack and stole into Steadman's lonely camp. His knife blade made a fatal slash across Steadman's throat. Just after dawn the next morning the first rays of the sun peeping over the top of a mountain to the east touched Steadman's face, which was set rigidly in death.

7

Night was closing in when Moran reached the livery barn in Lodgepole. He stabled his horse, went along the street to the diner located near the bank, and ate a good meal. His hunger sated, he turned his thoughts to duty and went to the hotel to see Mrs Rogers. At the reception desk he was told that she was in the hotel dining room having supper with Byron Slessor. Moran went to the doorway, peeped into the dining room, and saw Mrs Rogers seated at a table with Slessor. He departed, deciding to talk to her later.

He went on to the law office where he found Mike Colton, the day jailer, sitting at Steadman's desk.

'The sheriff rode out to check on horse-stealing at the Rafter O,' Colton told him. 'He won't be back until

tomorrow at the earliest. The deputy went out to the Rafter O yesterday — they lost about twenty horses — and he ain't come back, so Steadman has gone to look for him.'

'I'll come back tomorrow and talk to the sheriff,' Moran said. 'It was nothing important.'

He departed and went along the sidewalk to Brannigan's saloon. Full darkness had fallen and shadows were thick along the street. He paused on the sidewalk and looked around. The town seemed unnaturally quiet, although a buzz of conversation and laughter came from the saloon. He guessed there was more noise when the soldiers from the fort were allowed into town. He thrust open the batwings and entered the saloon, pausing again just inside to check his surroundings.

More than a dozen men were present, most of them bellied up to the bar, where Brannigan and his bartender, Sharkey, were busy serving and chatting to their patrons. Moran

glanced at six men playing poker at a table in a far corner, and his teeth clicked together when he recognized Gaines, the gambler, sitting in the game, his facial bruises showing livid in the bright lamplight. Moran shook his head as he considered, and went to the bar.

Brannigan, his forehead beaded with sweat, came along the bar. His face was expressionless, his eyes hard and glinting.

'I reckon you're the only soldier in town,' he commented. 'The off-limits order is killing my business. What'll you have to drink? It's on the house,'

'You shouldn't permit cheating in here,' Moran replied. 'I see your pet gambler is still in business. Listening to Slessor this afternoon, I reckoned Gaines would be long gone by now.'

'I'll get rid of him as soon as I can get hold of another gambler.' Brannigan grimaced. 'Do you want a drink?'

'Make it a beer,' Moran responded.

He turned his attention to the corner

table and decided to watch the poker game. When his beer arrived he picked it up, carried it across to Gaines's table, and watched the play, occasionally sipping a mouthful of beer. Gaines looked up and met his eyes, and it was the gambler who dropped his gaze first. Several minutes later Gaines threw in his cards, collected the money lying before him, and pushed away from the table.

'Count me out,' he said curtly. 'It's time for supper. I'll be back later.'

He met Moran's level gaze as he turned away, and Moran saw hostility in the dark eyes. Gaines crossed to the bar, spoke to Brannigan, who nodded and then departed. Moran went back to the bar, finished his beer and walked to the batwings. He had some straight talking to do to Mrs Rogers.

The moment he stuck his nose outside he realized he had made a mistake. He was silhouetted in the doorway, and sprang lithely to his left, heading for the shadows. As he moved

he heard a pistol fire three quick shots, and heavy echoes blasted around the street. One of the slugs tugged at his hat brim, and Moran threw himself full length to the sidewalk, jerking out his pistol as he hit the dusty boards. He twisted around to get a look in the direction from which the shots had come, and saw the flash of a gun wink and die in the shadows across the street.

Yellow lamplight shafted across the sidewalk from the big front window of the saloon, throwing an impenetrable barrier of brilliance into Moran's eyes. He sprang to his feet and dashed into the street to cross to the dark side, and was aware of more shots coming at him from the impenetrable gloom. He tripped over the edge of the opposite sidewalk and went down full length, landing heavily. The gun shooting at him was situated in an alley opposite the saloon, and more lead crackled through the shadows in a deadly attempt to nail him.

He triggered his Colt, sending an accurate group of shots at the alley mouth. The opposing gun shut down instantly. Moran held his fire and listened to the echoes fading away. He made no attempt to go after the ambusher because all the odds were against him, and he wondered if Gaines was responsible for the attack. He got to his feet, holstered his gun, and went swiftly along the sidewalk until he was opposite the diner. He crossed the street, entered the diner, and paused to look around the interior. Most of the tables were occupied by diners having supper, and he saw Gaines seated alone in a corner.

Moran heaved a sigh, certain that Gaines could not have ambushed him, but that was not to say the gambler had not paid someone else to handle the chore. He crossed to Gaines's table and looked down at him. Gaines did not change his expression. Both his hands were on the table in plain view.

'You got a problem, Captain?' he

demanded. 'You look like you've been rolling in the dust.'

'It was nothing I couldn't handle,' Moran replied. 'Are you carrying a gun?'

Gaines smiled. 'I'd feel undressed without one.' He reached into an inner pocket in his jacket, but halted the movement with his hand out of sight. 'I'll use my forefinger and thumb,' he added, and when Moran nodded he drew out a .41 derringer and laid it on the table. 'I expect you'd like to check it,' he continued. 'Go ahead and take a look.'

Moran picked up the small gun and sniffed at the muzzle. The weapon had not been fired recently. He placed it back on the table and turned away without another word. He left the diner and eased out to the sidewalk to go on to the hotel. He entered, and as he reached the reception desk, Mrs Rogers emerged from the dining room, followed by Slessor. Moran saw the woman's expression change when she

caught sight of him. She had been smiling at Slessor, but her pleasure turned to something less pleasant and she sighed heavily. Slessor paused by her side, permitting a grimace of annoyance to flit across his fleshy face when he saw Moran.

'I've timed my arrival just right,' Moran greeted with a smile.

'You're not going to bother Mrs Rogers with more questions, are you?' Slessor demanded.

'I'm afraid that's just what I aim to do. It will be better for all concerned if I get my job done as quickly as possible. Don't you agree, Mrs Rogers?'

'I don't know what else I can tell you, but if you think I can help your investigation then I'll be only too pleased to cooperate, Captain.' She turned to Slessor with a dismissive smile on her lips. 'I'll see you in the morning, Byron.'

'Come to my office when you and the captain have finished,' Slessor said eagerly.

'Thank you, but I have a headache which can only get worse. I'll talk to Captain Moran, and when he leaves I shall have to rest.'

Slessor scowled. 'Don't give her a hard time, Captain,' he warned.

'The way I react to Mrs Rogers will depend on her attitude,' Moran replied.

Slessor departed and Mrs Rogers looked around. She pointed to two chairs in a corner.

'We can sit over there,' she suggested.

Moran accompanied her across the lobby and waited until she had seated herself before pulling a chair round so that he could watch the street door. He sat down.

'I returned to the fort earlier and resumed my investigation into your husband's murder,' he commenced.

'And you have, no doubt, learned a great deal about me.'

Moran watched her face, able to see that she was instantly on the defensive, and there was a trace of emotion in her eyes which he assumed was fear.

'I learned a great deal about a number of persons,' he countered. 'What I want to ask you is, did your husband have any enemies?'

'You mean apart from the man who killed him. Quite a number, I should think, although I can't pinpoint anyone. But Tom was a bully and a cheat. He watered the beer, and overcharged for everything he sold. There were always complaints about the way he handled the business. I expect every soldier at the fort had bad feelings about him.'

'I'm looking for a motive for murder,' said Moran sharply, 'and I don't regard beer being watered as a reason for a man being killed.'

'They say Green killed my husband over a bottle of whiskey.'

'I arrested Green and brought him back. He insisted that he was innocent, and said he could prove it.'

'Don't all killers say that when captured?' she countered.

'In Green's case, I have a sneaking feeling he was telling the truth.'

'He is a hard man and holds a grudge very well.'

'You saw Green in town a number of times,' Moran mused.

'I never made a secret of my associations. Tom and I had a mutual agreement. We went our separate ways with no questions asked, so anything I did had no effect on our relationship.'

'And there were other soldiers in your life,' Moran said.

'And other men who were not soldiers,' she admitted with a faint smile. 'You saw one of them this evening. Slessor wants to marry me when Tom's murder fades into the background.'

'It is likely that every man you associated with had a motive for killing your husband, and Green was one of them.'

'You have been busy. Who has been telling tales about me?'

'Not tales — the truth, I suspect.'

'Have you questioned Green about our relationship?'

'Not yet.' Moran was not ready to divulge the news that Green was dead.

'The night he was killed, Tom told me he was having some trouble. It was before Green asked for a bottle of whiskey. I heard about that, too. Green was a drunkard, did you know?'

'I've had conflicting statements about that. One source said he was a drunkard and another said he hardly ever drank. It all depends on the point of view, I suppose.'

'Green tried to keep that knowledge to himself. He was very good at covering up, among other things.'

'He would have to be, meeting another man's wife secretly.' Moran began to grow impatient, aware that he was not going to get much help from this woman. He would have to drag every bit of information from her. 'If you name the men you have kept company with recently, I can try to eliminate them from my investigation. I need to check on everyone who might have had a motive for

killing your husband.'

'I won't do that,' she replied, shaking her head emphatically. 'If I thought one of them had anything to do with Tom's death then I'd tell you his name, but I believe Green killed my husband, and that's as far as I can go to help you.'

Moran got to his feet. He looked down into her face and she met his gaze impassively. He nodded.

'Thank you for your patience. I shall probably have to see you again as my investigation progresses.'

'I shall be pleased to see you at any time, Captain,' she replied. 'I hope you are successful with your inquiries.'

He left her, aware that she would not want the truth of her past to be revealed. He went into the hotel bar, bought a beer, and sat at a small table to consider what he had learned so far. As yet, he had too many suspects, and no clear idea how to whittle them down. He was beginning to think that Green did not commit suicide — there was no way he could have obtained a

rope, and, in that case, someone had murdered the deserter. That gave him three suspects: Sergeant Buller, Corporal Bessey, and Trooper Johnson. Sergeant Buller had been alone in the guardhouse with the prisoner so he'd had a good opportunity to kill Green.

He pushed all thoughts of the case into the background of his mind and considered the shooting which had been directed at him. Obviously Gaines had not handled it, but the gambler could have paid someone to attempt it. He shook his head. There was an alternative which he had to consider. A soldier could have been responsible for the shooting. If his investigation was getting too close for comfort to one of those he had already questioned — a man wanting to conceal murder — then he had to expect a violent reaction. He decided to concentrate on examining Buller, Bessey and Johnson.

It was unfortunate that Sheriff Steadman had left town, for the

lawman might have some knowledge of whom Mrs Rogers had been seeing around town. Moran left the hotel and went back to the saloon. He was wondering who had paid Adam Pyke to do a special job — shooting Colonel Denton. And why had John Benn gone along with Pyke to commit murder? The questions needing answers seemed endless, and Moran made an effort to control his impatience. If Green had not died, this investigation would have moved effortlessly to a conclusion. As it was, he had to dig into the past with the help of those who had been in a position to watch events unfolding before the murder of Tom Rogers.

Brannigan was talking to a small group of men bellied up to the bar, but he left them when he saw Moran and came along the bar, his expression suggesting that he was afraid someone would accost Moran and pass on some information.

'Would you like another drink, Captain?' Brannigan asked.

'No thanks. I'm after information, and perhaps you can help me.'

'I'm always ready to help the law, even if it's military law. What's on your mind?'

'I need to get some background information on several soldiers. Trooper Green in particular, and also those men who associated with him.'

'I knew Green well,' Brannigan said without hesitation. 'He was always in here. The saloon was like a second home to him.'

'Did he have a problem with drink?'

'Some would say so, but I never saw him the worse for wear because of it.'

'Did he gamble much?'

'If he wasn't propping up the bar then he was sitting in a game of poker. He spent all his off-duty hours in here. I could do with a few like him right now.'

'I heard he incited the trouble when Gaines was caught cheating.' Moran watched Brannigan's eyes, looking for the first flicker of a lie.

'He was the one who caught Gaines cheating, and did what any man would do. Gaines made it worse. The trouble got out of hand, and there was talk of lynching Gaines. There were around a dozen troopers in here at the time, and Sheriff Steadman had his work cut out to cool the situation.'

'Can you name any soldier that Green had as a friend?'

'Green was usually with a corporal. They were a familiar sight around here. The corporal's name is Bessey. He was a good influence on Green — steered him clear of a lot of trouble.'

'Thanks.' Moran turned away.

'Any time, Captain,' Brannigan replied, and went back along the bar.

Moran walked to the batwings, but paused and turned back into the saloon. There was a side door halfway along the room that gave exit to an alley. He went to it and departed quickly, stepping out into deep shadow and pausing to listen intently and to scan the shadows. The silence in the

alley pressed in around him like a blanket. He edged towards the main street, his right hand down on the butt of his holstered gun, ready for an ambush.

He breathed easier when he reached the sidewalk, and slid out of the alley into more shadows. He wondered who had ambushed him earlier. He needed a breakthrough, and the easiest way of getting one was to catch someone who was trying to kill him. He half-hoped someone would make another try for him.

When he was satisfied that no trouble awaited him he moved to his right and headed for the livery barn, deciding to head back to the fort to ask more questions of Corporal Bessey. He needed to know the names of the other two men who were under open arrest for taking part in the trouble with Gaines, and he considered putting pressure on Bessey in an attempt to lever information out of him.

He was hair-triggered when he

entered the stable. A single lantern cast dim light over a limited area, and heavy shadows blocked off the corners of the big barn. He prepared his horse for travel and, as he led it outside, a shadow moved on his right and a voice spoke softly. Moran was startled, and his gun appeared in his hand so fast he almost squeezed the trigger before he was able to control the movement.

'Hey, hold it!' the voice exclaimed. 'I'm Otis Jary, the livery man. You're the provost captain who was with the sheriff earlier, ain't you? I've got some information for you.,

'Don't sneak up on a man like that,' Moran replied, breathing deeply. 'You could get yourself killed.'

'I recognized you. Didn't you see me?'

'What do you want? I'm in a hurry to get back to the fort.'

'There's supposed to be an off-limits rule for soldiers, ain't there? Well, I saw a soldier come into town about an hour ago. He was in uniform.'

'Where is he?' Moran asked, instantly interested.

'He didn't leave his horse in here. I saw him put it in the timber yard opposite. He walked along the street and disappeared in the shadows.'

'Did you get a good look at him?'

'No. It was too dark. He came back after there was some shooting along the street, got his horse, and rode out, probably heading back to the fort. He was in such a hurry to get out of town I reckoned he was involved in the shooting. You better watch out he ain't along the trail waiting for you to show up.'

'Thanks for the information,' Moran said.

He led his horse outside, and relief filled him when he was in the saddle and riding out of town. He wondered if the soldier had been the ambusher. He had been thinking that Gaines organized the ambush. He considered the shooting. If a soldier had been intent on killing him then his motive had to be

the investigation that was being made into the sutler's murder. Someone was trying to smother the truth, which was still well hidden.

Moran relaxed a little as he followed the trail. He gave more thought to what he had learned about the situation. He always kept an open mind, but realized his instincts were pushing him in directions not indicated by the evidence. He was not so sure that Green had murdered Tom Rogers, but if he had, then the motive had to do with Mrs Rogers and not a bottle of whiskey.

He was jerked from his thoughts by his horse snorting and putting its ears forward. Moran peered ahead. The shadows were deceptive, but he caught a glimpse of a rider motionless on the trail. He reached for his pistol.

'Declare yourself,' he called sharply.

There was no reply. He could see the man was in uniform, and he watched keenly for sudden movement. There was none. The man was already

holding his pistol in his hand, and Moran, alerted by the silence, kicked his feet clear of his stirrups and hurled himself sideways out of his saddle. A pistol blasted the silence even as he moved, and he felt the burn of a bullet across his left hip. A gun flash cut through the darkness and echoes reverberated through the night.

Moran hit the trail on his right shoulder and rolled swiftly, expecting more shooting. He swung up his gun and fired as the muzzle covered the motionless figure. The gun flash dazzled his eyes and he blinked furiously. When his pupils had readjusted he was able to see clearly that the rider was pitching out of his saddle. Echoes growled in the distance.

He got to his feet. His horse had skittered away several yards, but now stood motionless. He went to where the soldier lay inert, and covered the figure with his gun. He saw a pistol lying close to the man's right hand and kicked it out of reach. A sigh escaped him as he

dropped to one knee beside the figure.

He could see a corporal's stripes on the man's sleeve, and a pang darted through him as he feared the worst. This could be Corporal Bessey, and most of his hopes concerning a quick wind-up to the investigation were centred in the man. He holstered his gun and felt for a match. By the aid of its tiny glow he looked at the face of the groaning man and recognized Bessey; he felt a pang of disappointment as he grasped the man's shoulder and shook it. He could see blood on Bessey's chest and realized the wound was serious.

'Bessey,' he said sharply. 'Can you hear me? This is Captain Moran. What are you doing out here? Were you waiting for me?'

Bessey groaned. The match burned down and was extinguished. Moran blinked and his sight slowly returned to normal in the gloom.

'Were you shooting at me in town, Corporal?' he demanded.

Bessey groaned again and stirred. 'I

knew you were trouble when I first saw you at the fort,' he muttered hesitantly. 'I knew you'd get at the truth. I had to stop you, so I sneaked into town and laid for you, but you were too good for me. And I tried for you again out here. Now you've done for me so it doesn't matter. And I'm not guilty of anything. I'll tell you this, Captain: Green didn't kill Rogers, and he didn't hang himself.'

'Tell me more,' Moran urged. 'Come on, Corporal, open up and give me the facts. Who killed Rogers, and who murdered Green?'

He waited for Bessey to reply but there was no response. Moran shook him by the shoulder; when there was no reaction he felt for the man's pulse. A sighed escaped him when he found nothing. Bessey was dead, and he had taken his knowledge with him across the Great Divide.

8

Moran checked his left hip and found a dribble of blood seeping from a bullet gouge in the flesh over the hip bone. It was not serious and he ignored it as he continued to the fort, leading the horse with Bessey's body hung over the saddle. A number of questions were hammering in his mind. Bessey had said Green did not murder Tom Rogers and had not committed suicide. Bessey had also asserted that he was not guilty of any crime, but if that was so then why had he ambushed Moran in town? And he had been desperate enough to make a second try on the trail. It was unfortunate that the man who could really help his investigation was dead, but his passing lessened the number of suspects to be considered, and Moran was keen to handle his next interview with Sergeant Buller.

On reaching the fort he rode across the parade ground to the troop office, where a light was still burning. There was no sign of a sentry outside. Moran dismounted and entered the office, hoping to find Top Sergeant Grimmer on duty; he was thankful to find him still at his desk. Grimmer got quickly to his feet and saluted.

'I'm relieved you're back, Captain,' Grimmer said. 'We've had some trouble here. Trooper Johnson was found dead in his quarters about two hours ago. He'd been stabbed.'

'Johnson?' Moran considered for a moment. 'He was on duty with Corporal Bessey when Green was placed in the guardhouse.'

'That's right, sir. The other thing is, Corporal Bessey cannot be found on the post.'

'I've brought him in,' Moran said, and watched the top sergeant's expression change when he narrated the incidents that had occurred in town and on the trail.

'Have you any idea what's going on, sir?' Grimmer asked. 'Why would Bessey attack you, Captain?'

'I don't know why, but I have a suspicion, and a lot of questions to ask. I need to talk to Sergeant Buller now.'

'Buller is not on the post at the moment, Captain. When Johnson was found dead we looked for Bessey and could not find him.

'So Sergeant Buller rode out to look for Bessey.' Moran mused.

'How'd you know that, Captain?' asked Grimmer, looking puzzled.

'It was just an inspired guess.' Moran suppressed a sigh.

'Buller took two troopers with him. He probably rode into town to the house where there's a woman Bessey was planning to marry.'

'I'll return to town immediately and see what I can learn,' Moran decided. 'Can you put a name to the woman Bessey knows?'

'She's Kate Donovan. Her father owns the timber mill in town. They live

in a big house opposite the livery barn.'

'Who are the two men Sergeant Buller took with him?'

'Troopers Levin and Tolliver, sir,' Grimmer said.

Moran turned to the door, then paused. 'Have Bessey's body taken care of,' he said. Grimmer nodded. 'I'll write up my report when I get back.'

He departed, and rode out for Lodgepole, his thoughts busy as he covered the five miles to the town, his mind whirling with conjecture. The situation was tearing itself apart and he had to try to match the sudden increase in pace. He needed to get hold of Buller, the only one of the three policemen who'd had the opportunity to kill Green in the guardhouse.

When he reached town he put his horse in the livery barn. There was no sign of Otis Jary, for which he was thankful, and he crossed the street to a big house standing beside the timber yard. Lights were showing in several windows, and he knocked at the door

and waited impatiently for a reply. The door was opened by a tall, thickset man of around forty, who gazed at Moran, his manner belligerent.

'What the hell do you want?' he demanded in a furious tone.

'What's your name?' Moran countered. 'By the tone of your voice I'd guess it is John Pig!'

The man clenched his big hands, then made a visible effort to control his temper.

'I'm Mike Donovan,' he said more reasonably. 'I apologize for letting my anger show — a family matter, you understand.'

'I'm Provost Captain Slade Moran and I'm investigating a murder and the trouble between the soldiers at the fort and certain individuals in town. I'd like to talk to Miss Kate Donovan.'

'If it's to do with Corporal Bessey then you'll be wasting your time,' Donovan said through his teeth. 'I've just finished laying down the law to Kate and she's finished with Bessey,

although she hasn't accepted the fact yet.'

'She is finished with him. Bessey is dead.'

Donovan opened his mouth to reply, and then his teeth clicked together. He stared at Moran in silence, his mouth slowly gaping open in shock.

'Dead?' he muttered. 'What happened? There was a sergeant and two troopers here about half an hour ago, asking after him, and they never mentioned his death.'

'They didn't know about it. I need to locate that sergeant. Have you any idea where he went when he left here?'

Donovan shook his head. 'I was busy trying to talk some sense into my daughter. You'd better come in if you want to talk to her.'

Moran removed his hat and stepped into a short passage. The first door on the right stood half-open, and he could see a young woman in the room, sitting in an easy chair beside an empty grate. Donovan led the way into the room and

Moran followed him, studying the girl, who was an attractive brunette with blue eyes and an angelic face. She wore a blue dress that enhanced the colour of her eyes.

'This is Captain Moran, Kate,' Donovan said. 'He wants to talk to you about Bessey.'

'I haven't seen him recently,' she replied, 'which I told the sergeant who called. And from what my father says, I shan't be allowed to see him again.'

'I have some bad news for you,' Moran said softly. 'It's about Corporal Bessey. I'm sorry to have to tell you that he's dead.'

Kate Donovan sprang to her feet, her expression changing. 'Did you know about this, Dad?' she demanded. 'Is that what the sergeant told you when he came?'

'No, Kate. Apparently the sergeant didn't know about Bessey when he called here.'

'What happened to him?' she asked Moran.

'He unsuccessfully ambushed me in town earlier, and I killed him when he tried again on the trail to the fort. I'd have liked to take him alive but he died in the shooting.'

'Why would he want to kill you?' Donovan demanded as Kate dropped back into her chair and buried her face in her hands.

'That's the question I'd like answered.' Moran shook his head. 'I'm hoping Sergeant Buller will be able to give me a reason — when I catch up with him.'

'I heard tell Buller was the latest soldier seeing the widow of the sutler who was killed at the fort,' Donovan mused. 'She's been seen around with more than one soldier recently, and it's common knowledge in town that there was trouble between the sutler and some of the soldiers because he objected to his wife's behaviour. I don't think you'll have to look far for the killer of Tom Rogers.'

'Thanks for the information,' Moran

said. 'I'm sorry to be the bearer of bad news.'

'It wasn't bad as far as I'm concerned,' Donovan said. 'I'll show you out, Captain.'

Moran turned to leave. He stood in the shadows, considering what he had learned. So Sergeant Buller was one of several soldiers who had been keeping company with Mrs Rogers. He made his way to the hotel, moving carefully along the street.

* * *

Sergeant Buller was troubled as he rode into Lodgepole with two of his closest associates, Levin and Tolliver. He had to find Bessey and kill him before Captain Moran could get to him. With Bessey dead the death of Johnson could be placed on Bessey's shoulders. Buller was at the centre of a ruthless reign of domination at the fort which had expanded from a few brutal incidents in the guardhouse against unfortunate

soldiers to outright murder in maintaining the rule of fear and violence which he had created.

He had killed Tom Rogers in a showdown over Mrs Rogers, and framed Green with the crime, telling the unfortunate trooper his only chance of survival was to desert. But Moran had brought Green back, and Buller, in a sweat of desperation, killed Green in his cell and arranged the murder to look like suicide. Corporal Bessey and Trooper Johnson had been unwilling accessories — having been drawn long before into Buller's web of deceit and violence — but with Moran's arrival the situation had changed. Moran looked like a man who would get at the truth unless he was stopped, and it was Buller's insistence that he should be killed by either Bessey or Johnson that had broken his hold on the situation. Bessey had gone reluctantly to murder Moran, but Johnson refused to have anything more to do with the brutal set-up — hence his demise.

Now Bessey had to die and shoulder the blame for Johnson's murder, unless Bessey succeeded in killing Moran, which seemed unlikely.

When they reached Lodgepole Buller led the way along the back lots to the rear of Brannigan's saloon. He had long ago formed a criminal association with the saloon man, and had been planning his own desertion for some weeks. Moran's arrival had precipitated his action and he now had cut himself loose from his army career, but needed to tie up some loose ends.

'We'll leave our horses back here,' Buller said to the two hardcase soldiers who had thrown in their lot with him. 'You two can take a look around for Bessey while I'm talking to Brannigan. You know what to do if you find Bessey. I want him dead. If you can't locate him then come and tell me, and if you set eyes on that long-nose captain then put him down, but good. Have you got that?'

'Sure thing,' Tolliver said. 'I only saw

the captain briefly at the fort this morning, but I'll know him if I see him again.'

Buller watched them disappear into the alley beside the saloon. He trusted them, and went to the rear door of the saloon, which opened to his touch. He entered quietly, made his way to the side door of the office, and tapped on the pine woodwork. A chair scraped inside the office, and a moment later the door was opened and Brannigan, gun in hand, peered out at him.

'Have they lifted the out-of-bounds rule?' Brannigan demanded.

'Not yet.' Buller stepped forward and Brannigan eased aside to permit the big sergeant to enter. 'I'm on duty, and I've got a couple of men with me. I'm after Bessey, who's wanted for killing Johnson. Bessey came to town this afternoon to kill Moran, who turned up at the fort this morning with Trooper Green under arrest. Everything has gone wrong from that point. Has Moran been around here?'

'I've seen him.' Brannigan returned to his seat behind the desk. 'He's some kind of a one-man army. Jake Woodson was in here this afternoon with Del Manning and a guy named Gann. It seems Gann was a deserter from the army and Moran had lost him a year ago. Gann pulled his gun, thinking Moran had caught up with him, and Moran beat him to the draw and shot him dead. I never saw a faster draw. It was hell on wheels. The sheriff brought Moran in here. It looked like they'd teamed up. Since then, someone ambushed Moran on Main Street, but didn't kill him. The last I heard, Moran rode back to the fort. He's got to be put down, Buller, before we can get on with my business. You've got to make him your first job now you're here.'

'It'll be taken care of. Tolliver and Levin are with me. They're looking for Bessey now, and they'll kill Moran when they set eyes on him. I wanta get out of this stinking uniform, and then

I'll take a look around for Moran. You got Colonel Denton put away this morning. It looks like Major Hopwood will take over at the fort, and he's in your pocket. If I get Bessey and Moran your trail will be clear.'

'You and your two men can move into that apartment over the gun shop like we arranged,' Brannigan said. 'Play it quiet until you've got rid of the opposition, huh?'

'Don't worry about a thing.' Buller picked up a whiskey bottle on the desk and swigged from it. 'We've got the world by the tail with a downward pull. Give me the key to the apartment.'

Brannigan took the key out of his desk drawer and handed it over. 'You'll find everything you asked for in the apartment,' he said. 'Keep quiet around the place until our problems are settled.'

'Don't worry about a thing,' Buller said. 'I know how many beans make five. If Levin and Tolliver show up here looking for me then send them to the

apartment and tell them to lie low. I'll see them later. My first chore will be to kill Moran. He could ruin everything if I don't nail him quick.'

Brannigan walked to the back door with Buller when the sergeant departed, and was thoughtful as he returned to his office. Events were moving smoothly now, and after the bank robbery there would be nothing to stop him reaching for the moon and getting it.

* * *

Moran had the feeling that he was walking on broken glass as he went along Main Street to the hotel. He kept to the shadows, and checked every likely ambush spot as he moved. He stepped into the doorway of a gun shop and paused to study his shadowy surroundings. The street was quiet, with little movement by townsfolk. He eased out of cover and reached the alley beside the hotel, then stepped into cover again and waited several minutes,

watching the sidewalks, checking for furtive movement and looking for the gleam of lamplight on a drawn gun.

He had a feeling in the back of his mind that was all too familiar. There was danger for him in this town, and the knowledge sharpened his wits and instincts. He eased his weight off his left leg and the niggling pain in his wound lessened slightly. He'd had no time to see the local doctor and get his wound dressed. He needed to press on with his investigation and, at the moment Mrs Rogers seemed to hold the key to his success. With any luck, he might find Sergeant Buller with her.

Satisfied that he was not being stalked, Moran went on to the hotel. There was a tingle of anticipation between his shoulder blades as he stepped out of the darkness and entered the brightly lighted lobby. He moved quickly out of the doorway. There was no one at the reception desk so he strode to the stairs and ascended quickly. When he reached the door of

Mrs Rogers's room he grasped the handle with his left hand and turned it gently. The door opened to his touch. There was lamplight in the room. He entered swiftly.

Mrs Rogers was seated on a sofa. She sprang to her feet at his abrupt appearance, her mouth opening to scream. But her teeth clicked together when she recognized him, and annoyance replaced the fear on her face.

'What do you mean by bursting in here like that?' she demanded. 'You have no right to bother me again. I've told you all I know. You would be better employed hunting down the man who killed my husband, not harassing a defenceless woman.'

'Tell me who killed your husband and I'll pick him up,' Moran responded, closing the door and advancing into the room. 'You haven't been truthful in your answers to my previous questions, so we'll have to start again, and this time you will tell me the truth.'

'How dare you talk to me like that?

I'll see the sheriff about you. You're hounding me, Captain.'

'You sound quite convincing,' Moran said. 'It's a good act you've got there. I've learned since I spoke to you earlier that you have associated with the two soldiers I suspect of being involved in your husband's death — Trooper Green and Sergeant Buller. I don't believe Green killed Tom Rogers over a bottle of whiskey. It's more likely that Sergeant Buller killed him over you. So start telling me the truth.'

Mrs Rogers sat down heavily on the sofa and buried her face in her hands. Moran remained motionless for several moments, watching her, and when she did not show signs of recovering her poise he went to her side and placed a heavy hand on her shoulder. She started slightly at his touch, then lowered her hands and looked up at him, her face pale and her eyes dry.

'Help me,' she said harshly. 'I'm in such trouble I don't know which way to turn.'

'I can only help you if you tell me the truth about what happened just before and after your husband's death. Give me some facts to work on and I'll see that nothing bad happens to you unless you were actively involved in your husband's death. I'll arrest the guilty man and the case will be closed.'

He paused, and the silence in the room was vibrant as she gazed at him with wide, fear-filled gaze. She shook her head slowly. Tears shimmered in her eyes. When they began to roll down her cheeks she reached for a handkerchief and dabbed at her face. Moran was not touched by her distress. He waited, his face expressionless, and the minutes dragged by remorselessly.

'You have no idea of the situation that exists at the fort,' she said at length.

'Then tell me about it,' he urged.

'I daren't. If I uttered one word I would be killed like poor Tom was. You don't know what a monster the killer is. Every man at the fort is afraid of him.

He has killed before, and nothing could be proved against him.'

'Put a name to him,' Moran said. 'I know who you're talking about, but I need you to name him and give me proof of what he did.'

'Sergeant Buller!' Her voice was little more than a whisper, and she clutched her handkerchief with trembling fingers. 'He killed my husband, and then hounded poor Buster Green into deserting by rigging the evidence of Tom's murder so it appeared that Green killed him. He forced men to give false statements incriminating Green, and left Green with no alternative but to desert so he could be hunted down and killed for resisting arrest.'

'Who gave the false evidence?' Moran asked. 'Buller must have told you about it. I assume you had stopped seeing Green before your husband's death and were seeing Buller by then. When did you know Buller had killed your husband? Was it before or after the event?'

'Do you think I would have stood by and done nothing if I had known of Buller's intention to murder my husband?' she demanded. 'He told me about it after he had trapped me in his web of deceit and violence, and by that time I was unable to stand up to him. He even threatened to involve me in Tom's death if I attempted to reveal the truth. The way he explained it to me, I knew I wouldn't have a chance of clearing myself. He would have said I suggested that he kill Tom. But he made a mistake when he failed to find Green after he deserted. Green was supposed to desert, hide out near by and wait for Buller to go to him with money. But Green was not that stupid. He got out while he could.'

'And I caught Green, brought him back to the fort, and put him in Buller's guardhouse,' Moran said quietly. 'Thirty minutes later, he was dead.'

'Is Green dead?' she gasped. She

sprang to her feet and began to pace the room.

Moran moved to place himself between her and the door.

'I shan't try to run away,' she said harshly.

Moran did not reply. He watched her for several moments, and when her agitation showed no sign of easing he placed a hand on her arm and led her back to the sofa.

'Did Buller kill Green?' she demanded.

'I suspect Buller acted in panic when Green was thrust upon him without warning. He was unable to account for the rope Green was supposed to have used. Can you tell me about the false evidence Buller concocted to frame Green?'

'He used the regimental policemen who were under his command. Corporal Bessey told me he tried to do the right thing, but when he threatened to reveal the truth Buller cowed him into submissiveness.'

'Bessey tried to shoot me,' Moran said. 'I killed him to save myself.'

'Bessey is dead too?' Mrs Rogers started to her feet again. 'Buller said he would kill everyone if things started to go wrong, and it looks as if he's doing just that.'

'Buller doesn't know Bessey is dead, and is out looking for him with two men, Tolliver and Levin. I think they are in town right now, prowling around, but from what you've told me I can now take steps to apprehend them.'

'Do you think you can handle them alone?' she demanded. 'Buller is a killer, and those two men with him are no better. Buller hinted to me that he has friends here in town who are bad men. He didn't name them, but they are mixed up in lawlessness. There was talk of horse-stealing. That's the kind of men you've got against you, and you talk of arresting them as a matter of course.'

'That's the way I work,' Moran said easily. 'I need to get out there now and

do my job. But what shall I do with you in the meantime? I wouldn't want you to fall into Buller's hands, and I can't take a chance on you not running to him with a warning that I'm after him. I suppose I could put you in jail in protective custody until I've got Buller. Would you agree to go along with that?'

'I'll do whatever you decide,' she said. 'Just don't leave me alone here. If Buller is in town then he'll certainly come to see me, and after what you've told me I couldn't face him to save my life. He'll take one look at me and guess that I've talked about his activities. He'll kill me for sure.'

'Then let's go to the law office and I'll get you settled out of harm's way. I shall want a full statement from you as soon as possible.'

'I'll do anything you say now I've decided to tell the truth. But you need help to arrest Buller and those others.'

'Not if I take them separately,' Moran told her. 'Let's get moving.'

Mrs Rogers arose immediately and

walked to the door. Moran opened it for her, and she went out to the corridor. He followed her, paused to close the door, and heard her gasp. He looked up quickly as she turned and came back towards him. He side-stepped her, looked towards the head of the stairs, and set his right hand into motion when he saw Sergeant Buller coming along the corridor, in the act of drawing his army Colt.

9

Moran thrust Mrs Rogers aside as he drew his pistol. Buller had halted, his gun clearing leather. Moran's muzzle lifted swiftly. He sensed that he was a split second slower than the killer sergeant and hurled himself to the floor. He thumbed back his hammer. The two weapons blasted in a double thunderclap of noise. Muzzle flame spurted and smoke flared. Moran hit the floor hard, and heard the crackle of a closely passing slug in his right ear. He saw Buller jerk as hot lead bored into him. He staggered to the left and his shoulder hit the wall. He started to fall but made an effort and managed to remain standing.

Buller continued to work his gun, using two hands. Blood was showing on his shirt front at his left hip. Moran fired a second shot, aiming for the right

shoulder, aware that he had the edge. His slug hammered into Buller at the point where he aimed. Buller lost his grip on his gun, which thumped on the floor, and then he fell sideways against the wall and slid down into a crumpled heap beside the weapon. Moran went forward, covering the still figure. He kicked the discarded pistol out of reach of Buller's hand.

Moran's ears were protesting at the noise of the shooting. He glanced at Mrs Rogers, who was crouching on the floor, her hands over her ears, her eyes closed. Her lips were moving silently, as if she was praying. Moran checked Buller. He was unconscious, his face pale, and he was losing blood from his shoulder wound. Moran turned to Mrs Rogers.

'Let's get out of here,' he said. 'I'll get help for Buller shortly but first I want to see you secure.' He could hear heavy footsteps ascending the stairs from the lobby; he went to the top of the stairs and looked down. Slessor was coming,

and he halted abruptly when he saw Moran above him, gun in hand. 'Fetch the doctor in a hurry,' Moran called.

Slessor turned quickly and ran down the stairs. He hurried across the lobby and disappeared into the night. Moran turned to Mrs Rogers, who had not moved. She was badly shocked.

'Get up and come with me,' he rapped. She scrambled to her feet, swaying as if she'd had too much to drink. She came to him and he grasped her arm tightly. 'You're doing OK,' he observed. 'Come on.'

He held his pistol in his right hand. They descended the stairs in a rush and Moran kept going, mindful that Levin and Tolliver were somewhere around, probably looking for him, and he did not know them by sight. He pushed Mrs Rogers out through the street doorway and hurried her into the surrounding shadows, making for the law office. He could hear boots rapping the sidewalk as townsmen approached the hotel to check on the shooting.

Colton, the jailer, was standing in the doorway of the law office. He dropped a hand to the butt of his holstered pistol as Moran approached.

'Say, what's going on?' he demanded when he recognized Moran. 'I heard shooting. Was it in the hotel?'

'It's OK,' Moran said. 'I was attending to army business. Take Mrs Rogers into protective custody. Her life might be in danger. Put her in a cell and lock the door. I'll be back shortly with another prisoner.'

Colton escorted Mrs Rogers into the office and closed the door. Moran turned and hurried back to the hotel, keeping watch for uniformed figures. As he entered the lobby he saw Slessor and a tall man ascending the stairs. Several townsmen were standing at the bottom of the stairs, talking excitedly. They fell silent when Moran pushed through them.

'Has anyone seen two soldiers around town this evening?' he demanded.

'The town is out of bounds to

soldiers,' someone said.

'I saw a soldier a few minutes before the shooting,' another volunteered. 'He went into Brannigan's saloon as I came out.'

'There was a soldier at the livery barn thirty minutes ago,' said yet another. 'He looked like he was watching for someone. Don't forget their colonel was shot today.'

Moran ascended the stairs and found Slessor and the doctor beside Buller. Slessor looked at Moran as if he had never seen him before. His fleshy face was grey with shock, and his voice shook when he spoke.

'Where's Mrs Rogers?' he demanded.

'In a safe place,' Moran replied. 'How is Buller?'

'I'm Doc Yelding,' the tall man cut in. 'Who are you?'

'He's Captain Moran of the military police,' Slessor said quickly. 'He's handling the trouble we've been getting from the soldiers.'

Yelding, a tall, lean man in his fifties,

dropped to one knee beside the unconscious Buller and examined him. He grimaced when he looked up.

'I'll need to work on him before I can accurately judge his condition. Get some men to carry him over to my place.'

'See to it, Slessor,' Moran said. 'There's a crowd gathering in your lobby.'

Slessor looked as if he wanted to argue, but shrugged and hurried away. Moran heard him shouting to the crowd, and shortly four men came up the stairs, picked up Buller, and carried him away under the doctor's supervision. Moran followed them down to the lobby.

'I'll want him placed in the jail if you're able to save him,' Moran told the doctor. 'I'll be in the law office, so you can contact me there.'

He waited until the group had disappeared across the street and then stood in the shadows outside the hotel, looking around for signs of two men in

cavalry uniform. He wondered about Buller being out of uniform and where he had picked up civilian clothes. The thought struck him that perhaps Tolliver and Levin had got rid of their uniforms, and he felt that he was at a great disadvantage as he went along to the jail.

★ ★ ★

Del Manning lost no time in leaving the derelict ranch after killing Sheriff Steadman. He saddled his horse and rode north to meet up with Jake Woodson, It was close to midnight when he dismounted in a gully, knee-hobbled his horse, and made his way to a cave in the left-hand wall of the gully. It was a hideout he and Woodson had used several times, and he approached it cautiously, pausing near to the cave mouth to whistle and announce his presence. An answering whistle came to him and he went forward boldly, to be met by

Woodson's shadowy figure.

Starshine was reflected by the gun in Woodson's hand.

'Is that you, Del?' Woodson demanded.

'You'd be in a lot of trouble if it wasn't,' Manning replied.

'I was beginning to give up on you. Come in and have a cup of coffee. It's about time we pulled out for Lodgepole. We're picking up the bank dough around noon tomorrow, and we've got a long way to go. Did the sheriff show up looking for his deputy?'

'And how!' Manning laughed callously. 'I slit his throat while he slept. He never knew what killed him. What a way to go!'

'We should hit town after sunup,' Woodson mused. 'Brannigan will give us breakfast, then we'll go to the bank.'

'And you're of a mind to handle it like Brannigan says, huh?' Manning demanded. 'You're gonna hand the dough back to the banker.'

'I reckon there's a lot more dough to be made around Lodgepole, working

with Brannigan,' Woodson mused. 'If we find we're wrong we can always walk into the bank a second time and pick up the dough again. How does that sound?'

'Now you're talking, pard. Forget about the coffee. Let's hit the trail, and maybe I'll get a chance to finish the job I started on Moran. What have you done with the horses we picked up?'

'Snark and the others are running them north to Fort Frederick. The guys will be back at Owl Creek in a couple of weeks, and we'll meet up with them then.'

Woodson fetched his horse and prepared it for travel. When Manning had collected his mount they set off on the long ride to town.

★ ★ ★

Brannigan became nervous when he heard the shooting at the hotel and, learning that Moran had shot Buller, he became fearful. When Tolliver and

Levin walked into his office, still wearing their uniforms, he was relieved.

'I've learned that Buller is gonna be put behind bars when the doc has finished with him,' Brannigan said. 'You two go pick him up before Moran gets hold of him again and take him away from here. I don't want any trouble around town tomorrow, so get out and stay out for a few days.'

'Where can we take him?' Tolliver demanded. 'We can't go back to the fort. Heck, Levin and me can't even get out of our uniforms. What are we gonna do?'

'There's a room over the small bar at the other end of town,' Brannigan said. 'You know the place I mean — Duffey's Bar. Take Buller and keep him there until I get in touch. You two better stay out of sight. Forget about killing Moran. He'll be taken care of soon enough. Now get out of here and collect Buller from the doc's place.'

The two deserters departed and crossed the street to Doc Yelding's

office. When they entered Yelding was finishing his treatment of Buller.

'We're gonna take him back to the fort,' said Tolliver hastily.

'I got instructions from Captain Moran to haul him over to the jail,' Yelding replied.

'The captain's changed his mind. That's why we're here,' Tolliver insisted.

Doc Yelding shook his head. 'He can't be moved yet. He'll have to spend a couple of days here. You can tell Moran so.'

Tolliver and Levin withdrew with the intention of going to Duffey's Bar to lie low.

★ ★ ★

Moran prepared himself for a long night as he returned to the law office. Colton admitted him.

'Any idea when Sheriff Steadman will return?' Moran inquired.

Colton shook his head. 'There's no telling,' he replied. 'He could be gone

213

for days. I should have gone off duty hours ago, but I'm staying on duty until this trouble is settled.'

'I need to get a statement from Mrs Rogers.' Moran went through to the cells and found Mrs Rogers sitting on a bunk. She started up nervously when Moran walked in on her, and shook her head when he mentioned her statement.

'Not tonight,' she said instantly. 'I'm exhausted mentally and physically. It will have to wait until tomorrow.'

He knew by the tone of her voice that she would not cooperate until she decided the time was right. He left the office, intending to search for Tolliver and Levin. He stood in the shadows of a nearby alley-mouth, looking around the street, and was about to move on when he saw two soldiers emerging from the doctor's house. He drew his pistol when they came towards him, and drew back into the shadows as they passed, unaware of his presence. He heard one speak to the other.

'Ain't you gonna tell Brannigan about Buller? He'll need to know.'

'Not now,' the other replied. 'Let's get under cover before we run into Moran.'

Moran cocked his gun.

'You two men,' he called. 'I've got a gun on you. Halt and raise your hands.'

Tolliver and Levin halted instantly and their hands went up quickly. Moran approached and relieved them of their weapons.

'I'm Provost Captain Moran,' he told them. 'The town is off limits. Who are you and what are you doing here?'

When neither man replied, Moran continued:

'I assume you're Tolliver and Levin. You absented yourselves from Fort Collins without leave along with Sergeant Buller. I saw you emerging from the doctor's house, so you obviously know what's happened to Buller. I shot him for resisting arrest. You're standing outside the law office, so enter now and I'll follow. You'll be locked in cells until

215

I can get a military escort to take you back to the fort. Do you have any questions?'

'It looks like you got us flat-footed,' Tolliver said. He moved to his left and opened the door of the law office. He entered, followed by Levin. Moran stayed close behind them, ready for trouble, but they made no attempt to resist arrest. When he had locked them in separate cells; he confronted them.

'One of you mentioned telling Brannigan about Buller being shot,' he said. 'What did you mean by that? What has Brannigan to do with Buller?'

'You must have misheard,' Tolliver said. 'I don't recall saying or hearing anything like that. Who is Brannigan, anyway?'

Levin laughed as if Tolliver had made a joke. Moran regarded them for a moment and then turned away. He would let them sweat, would question them further when they were safely in the guard house at the fort. But he was intrigued by what he had overheard.

Mrs Rogers had said that Buller was associating with criminals in the town, and he would pass on that information when he saw the sheriff.

He chatted with Colton for a few minutes, then left the office to visit the doctor. Yelding was sitting at the desk in his office. Buller was lying heavily bandaged and unconscious on the examination couch.

'He shouldn't be moved until tomorrow at the earliest,' Yelding said. 'He won't regain consciousness for hours, and will be unable to move without assistance. You can leave him here until the morning.'

'In that case I'll ride back to the fort and get a military escort to come in for him,' Moran replied. He departed, and was on his way to the livery barn to get his horse when, on impulse, he turned into Brannigan's saloon. He was remembering that Jake Woodson and Del Manning had been in the saloon talking to Brannigan earlier; also he wanted to take another look at Gaines.

The saloon was busy. More than twenty men were either lined up at the long bar or seated at the scattering of small tables in the big room. Cigarette smoke was thick and voices were loud. Moran went to the nearest corner of the bar and let his gaze flit around. He saw Gaines back in his accustomed place at the corner table; five men were with him, each trying to beat the gambler at his own game.

Moran relaxed a little. He noted that Gaines was watching him intently. He had reckoned that Gaines was responsible for the ambush against him earlier until Bessey had made contact outside the town, and he recalled that Woodson, Manning and Gann had been in the saloon when Gann made his play and died for his action. His roving gaze picked out Brannigan, seated at a small table with two townsmen, talking seriously. Brannigan was facing Moran, his gaze intent, unwavering, fixed upon Moran like a rattlesnake watching its prey.

Moran turned away, deciding to return to the law office and remain there until morning. When he passed out of the saloon, Brannigan got up from his table and went back to where Gaines was seated. He motioned for the gambler to join him at the bar.

'Now's the time for you to kill Moran,' Brannigan said when Gaines joined him. 'He's just left, and you won't find a better time than now. Shoot him in the back.'

Gaines opened his mouth to protest, but the expression on Brannigan's face stopped him and he shrugged. He went to the batwings, pushed through them, and disappeared into the shadows. He spotted Moran's tall figure making its way along the sidewalk, and hurried to get within range, his derringer in his hand and murder in his heart.

Moran moved easily towards the law office. His thoughts were flitting across the broad lines of his case. Salient points presented themselves to be reconsidered, and generally he was

well pleased with the way his investigation was moving. He felt that he had the situation under control, aware that events concerning Brannigan and Woodson were not within his province. He could not interfere in civil law unless soldiers were involved, and with the out-of-bounds law imposed on the soldiery at the fort there was little danger of complications arising to distract him from his duty.

A tiny shiver suddenly made its presence felt between his shoulder blades and travelled through him like a kiss of death. Without thinking he stepped aside instantly into the dark, recessed doorway of a dress-shop, drew his pistol, and peered out to check his surroundings. He had been caught up in many life or death events during his career, and had come to rely implicitly on his sixth sense.

He looked towards the saloon and saw a dark figure approaching, which suddenly slipped into an alley mouth. A

moment later he saw a head appear and turn to survey the street. He cocked his gun and steadied his breathing. Some unfinished business was about to catch up with him. He remained in the doorway, waiting with the patience of a veteran campaigner, standing with only half his face exposed to enable one eye to watch his rear.

Minutes passed, and he continued to wait, aware that if he was the target of the man back there, then his would-be assailant should be getting impatient. Moments later he saw the figure emerge from the alley and continue along the sidewalk. Tension filled Moran, despite his experience in such situations. He moistened his lips and watched the man draw nearer. The shadows were too dense for him to make out details, and he prepared for action, watching for the first signs of hostility.

Moran moved back in the doorway until his left elbow made contact with the door of the shop. The man kept coming, and began to push into the

same doorway for cover, until he realized that Moran was there. Then he shied away like a nervous horse, and Moran saw his right elbow bend as if he was levelling a gun.

'Hold it,' Moran snapped. 'I've got you covered.'

Gaines froze. His gun was not lined up on Moran and he dared not make another movement. He raised both hands above his shoulders, and Moran glimpsed the small gun in Gaines's hand. He reached out swiftly and snatched it from the gambler's grasp.

'What are you doing with this in your hand?' Moran demanded. 'You were going to shoot me, huh?'

'No,' Gaines said. 'I was checking to see if it was fully loaded.'

'Let's go along to the law office and talk about it. I think you were planning to back-shoot me.'

Elroy Gaines began to protest but Moran pushed him out of the doorway and on to the sidewalk, jabbing the muzzle of his Army Colt against the

gambler's spine.

'You know the way,' Moran rapped. 'Get moving.'

'I swear I was not looking for you,' Gaines said. 'I have to be careful when I leave the saloon in case there are soldiers out here waiting to take a shot at me.'

They entered the law office. Moran searched Gaines, then took him through to the cells. Gaines protested vehemently but was put behind bars.

'I'm not satisfied with you,' Moran said. 'You followed me out of the saloon and I picked you up with a gun in your hand. So what were you going to do — pick your teeth with it? You're in a lot of trouble already, and you'll stay where you are until you can come up with a different reason for being behind me and holding a gun.'

'You can't arrest me,' Gaines protested. 'You've got no jurisdiction over civilians.'

'You've got a lot to learn about the law,' Moran told him. 'You'll stew in

there until the sheriff gets back. It'll be up to him what he does about you.'

He went back into the front office and Colton, drowsing at the desk, stirred, muttered unintelligibly, and settled down to sleep again. Moran heaved a sigh. It had been a long day. He dragged a chair up to the desk and sat down. He pulled the brim of his hat down over his forehead, closed his eyes, and slept.

* * *

Jake Woodson and Del Manning rode through the night towards Lodgepole. They were accustomed to riding back trails when most other folks were asleep, and the sun was adding golden fire to the eastern sky when they finally sighted the town. Manning stifled a yawn and eased himself in his saddle.

'Let's drop into the diner before we do anything else,' he suggested. 'My stomach has an idea that my throat's been cut.' He thought of Sheriff

Steadman and grinned. 'Now I know how that sheriff must have felt when I slit his throat.'

'We've got time on our hands now,' Woodson mused. 'We'll walk into the bank around noon.'

'So we can catch up on some sleep in the saloon, huh? Brannigan's got some spare rooms over the bar. Where do we head for after taking the dough out of the bank?' Manning once more thought about stealing the money and running.

'I ain't crossing any river until I come to it,' Woodson replied. 'Let's ride behind the saloon and leave our horses there. That livery man is too damn nosy for my liking. I reckon Brannigan will feed us.'

They skirted the main street and reached the rear of the saloon unseen.

* * *

Moran awoke with a start as the sun came up. He eased off the uncomfortable chair and stretched to get the kinks

225

out of his back and neck. Colton was seated at the other side of the desk, reading a newspaper. He grinned.

'I'll be going off duty shortly,' he said. 'Do you want breakfast for your prisoners?'

'I reckon I can let Mrs Rogers go this morning, and the soldiers will be going back to the fort as soon as I can arrange an escort for them. Gaines can stay where he is.'

'Do you think he was setting himself up to shoot you?'

'It looked that way. I didn't wait to find out. The sheriff will handle it when he gets back.'

Moran picked up the keys and went into the cell block. Gaines was asleep in his cell, as were Tolliver and Levin in theirs. Mrs Rogers was sitting on her bunk, looking as if she hadn't slept at all during the night. Moran unlocked the door of her cell.

'I think you'll be quite safe on the outside now,' he told her. 'Buller is helpless at the doc's house, and these

two soldiers will be going back to the fort under escort. I'll see you at the hotel later.'

He escorted Mrs Rogers out to the sidewalk and watched her head for the hotel. When she had disappeared inside he suppressed a sigh and went on to the diner. After he had eaten he went to the livery barn to check on his horse, and was leaving the building when the sound of approaching hoofs attracted his attention. He spotted a rider approaching from the direction of the fort, and his interest quickened when he saw the man's blue uniform.

He recognized Sergeant Grove, who reined in and saluted.

'You're early to meet the stagecoach, Sergeant,' Moran said.

'I've got some personal business in town to sort out before the stage arrives, Captain,' Grove replied.

'And I want you to return to the fort now, see Top Sergeant Grimmer, and tell him to arrange for an escort of six men and a sergeant to report to me

here in town. I have Sergeant Buller and Troopers Tolliver and Levin under arrest and need an escort to take them back to the fort. I'll be waiting at the law office. Make haste, Sergeant.'

Grove's face changed expression, but he made no comment, saluted again, and turned his horse instantly. He spurred the animal and set off at a fast run back the way he had come. Moran watched him until he was out of sight before turning to go on to the hotel. He was startled when Otis Jary, the livery man, emerged from the barn and called him.

'You asked yesterday about a blue-shirt rider on a white horse,' Jary said, 'and I just saw him. He rode past the corral out back with another guy as I was getting a sack of oats from my barn. I pegged him as a bad man soon as I saw him. He's got that look about him. In this business I get to see all kinds, and he's a wrong 'un if ever I saw one.'

'Where did he go?' Moran demanded.

'No further than the back of the saloon. I stood and watched him, knowing you'd be interested. The two of them went into the saloon by the back door. I reckon they're up to no good, if you ask me. I usually tell the sheriff when I spot something going on, but he ain't in town right now, and they tell me you're a military policeman. I've had doubts about Brannigan, the saloon man, for a long time; like I told the sheriff.'

'Thanks,' Moran said. 'I'll look around. I'll know that man in the blue shirt if I set eyes on him again — and his horse.'

'They put their horses in the saloon's barn out back. Looks like they're planning on sticking around for a spell and don't want anyone to know they're here. But they can't hide from me. I'm watching for trouble all the time.'

Moran nodded and walked through the barn to the back door. He paused by the corral out back and studied the empty lots. There were several buildings

round about — a big barn for the general store, a mortuary at the back of the undertaker's place where the dead of the town spent their last days before interment, and a profusion of sheds and cabins, most of them inhabited by the poorer folks of the town.

Stillness embraced the early morning, and there was a silence that was never apparent when townsfolk were on the move. The sun was beginning to gather its strength, and Moran peered around, not taking the peacefulness at face value. His right hand rested on the butt of his holstered gun as he looked for sunlight glinting on a naked weapon and listened for unnatural sound, like a stealthy footfall as an assailant closed in for the kill.

He moved on to the barn behind the saloon, watching the rear of the building for movement. He slid in against the barn, paused when he heard horses moving inside, and went to the rear. A back door stood ajar. He approached it, hand on gun butt, and

entered the barn, ready to flow into action at the slightest alarm. Then he halted and raised his hands shoulder high, for rising up from behind several bales of straw in a corner was a grinning Del Manning with a pistol in his right hand, its muzzle levelled at Moran's chest.

10

Del Manning stalked forward, snaked Moran's gun out of its holster, and moved around behind him, He flipped Moran's hat off his head and struck quickly with the barrel of his gun, slamming heavy metal against the unprotected skull. Moran dropped to his knees as if the roof of the barn had fallen in on him. He pitched forward on to his face and remained motionless.

'I had a nasty feeling you'd be sneaking around,' Manning said, kicking Moran in the ribs. 'Come on. Get up. You ain't hurt — yet. But you've got it coming, sure as hell! I liked Gann but you never gave him a chance yesterday; so I'm gonna make you sweat blood before you get your come-uppance.'

Moran opened his eyes. His vision was blurred, and the interior of the barn was spinning. There was a buzzing

in his ears, and Manning's voice seemed to be distorted. His senses cleared slowly and he finally looked up at the killer, who was grinning widely, the gun in his hand rock steady.

'Let's go into the saloon and talk to Brannigan and Woodson,' Manning said, his grin fading. 'Make it quick. I ain't got all day. Brannigan was talking about you. It seems his pet gambler left the saloon last night to put you out of circulation and didn't return. So what happened to him, huh?'

Moran pushed himself into a sitting position. He picked up his hat and put it back on his head. He saw four horses inside the barn, and recognized a grey as being the horse his attacker had ridden the day before. He wondered why he hadn't identified Manning earlier. He got to his feet and pretended to be more dazed than he was. But Manning was not fooled and did not come within an arm's length.

'We'll go into the saloon now,' Manning said. 'Don't try to get smart. I

know all the tricks, and then some. Brannigan's got some questions to ask you.'

Manning moved unsteadily out of the barn and walked across to the rear door of the saloon. Manning followed him closely and they entered the building. Brannigan was standing in the doorway to his office; his face took on a bleak expression when he saw Moran.

'What gives?' he demanded when he saw Manning behind Moran.

'He was snooping around your barn so I brought him in for a talk. When you've finished with him I'll take him back out to the barn and kill him.'

'No shooting around here this morning,' Brannigan warned.

'You worry too much.' Manning grinned. 'I'll slit his throat like I killed that nosy sheriff yesterday.'

'You killed Steadman?' repeated Brannigan in horror. He turned in the doorway and spoke to Woodson, who was inside the office. 'What's going on, Jake? Did you know about the sheriff?'

'I told Del to do it,' Woodson replied. 'We don't pussyfoot around in our business, Cully. The deputy showed up at Owl Creek and Del killed him. I moved the horses out to the mountain meadow, and left Del to watch for the sheriff. Sure enough, Steadman rode in after dark, so he joined the deputy. Now it looks like we got a problem with this soldier boy.'

'He's no problem,' said Manning.

'You better hogtie him and we'll keep him here until after you get the bank dough,' Brannigan mused. 'And you can take him along with you when you ride out with the dough. Don't kill him around here. When he doesn't turn up at the fort there'll be a big search for him, and I don't want him found anywhere in town.'

'No sweat,' Manning said. 'You got some rope?'

Brannigan produced a length of rope and Manning bound Moran hand and foot and tied him to a chair in the office. He used Moran's yellow

neckerchief as a gag, and grinned as he stepped back to inspect his handiwork. Brannigan confronted Moran.

'You shot Buller last night,' he accused.

'It's my duty to shoot deserters who resist arrest,' Moran replied.

'And you jailed Tolliver and Levin, so I heard,' Brannigan continued.

'We can turn them loose if you need them,' Woodson said. 'But let's have some breakfast first. We'll go to the diner. You'll be safe enough with Moran hogtied, but we'll stick him in your barn if you'd prefer it.'

'I like that idea.' Brannigan nodded. 'And don't forget to take him out of town when you've picked up the bank dough. Tate said to go into the bank at noon, so do like he says and it will go off without a hitch. But go to the law office after breakfast and bust Tolliver and Levin out. Tell them to pick up Buller and get him out of town.'

Manning untied Moran's legs and he

and Woodson escorted Moran out to the barn. When he was left alone, Moran set about trying to escape, but soon realized that Manning knew a thing or two about tying knots.

He was shocked by what he had heard in the saloon. Sheriff Steadman and his deputy had been murdered by Manning, and the bank was to be robbed at noon. He redoubled his efforts to escape, but no amount of struggling had any effect on the knots. Time passed, and a sense of desperation filled him. Sweat beaded his forehead, and was running freely down his face when he finally admitted that he was beaten. He could not loosen his bonds.

A sound outside the barn alerted him and he froze. A shadow passed by a window in the side of the barn, and moments later the back door creaked open. Moran drew a deep breath as he waited, expecting to see Del Manning, but sudden hope flared inside him when he recognized Otis Jary pausing

in the doorway. The livery man was carrying a shotgun, and paused warily on the threshold as he looked around.

Moran tried to make a sound, but was half-choked by the neckerchief stuffed into his mouth. He was afraid Jary would miss him. But Jary came across and set down his shotgun.

'I told you they were up to no good,' he said, 'and it was a good thing I've been watching them. I saw that little guy take you into the back of the saloon with a gun in your back and then bring you out again hogtied.'

He freed Moran quickly, pulled a pistol out of the holster nestling on his right thigh and stuck the weapon into Moran's ready hand.

'That's all I can do for you,' he said, picking up his shotgun. 'What you do about them now is your business. I ain't a fighting man, and I'm getting outa here.'

'Thanks for your help,' Moran said. 'I can handle it now. I'll return your gun to you later.'

Jary scuttled away. Moran checked the pistol, and paused when his senses suddenly swirled. He leaned against a wall, fearing he would lose his balance. His head was aching, and a large bump had formed on his head from Manning's blow. He pushed back his shoulders, summoned up his determination, walked out of the barn and crossed to the back of the saloon, ready for what he had to do.

* * *

Sergeant Grove was in a sweat by the time he reached the fort. He was in a bad mood because Moran had sent him back for an escort. Before he left the fort he had decided to face Myron Tate in a showdown over Nora; he had worked out what he wanted to say to the banker, and he was fired up for the confrontation. He dismounted in front of headquarters and hurried into the building, reported to Top Sergeant Grimmer, and was on his way back out

of the fort within five minutes. He did not spare his horse on the ride back to Lodgepole.

He reached town again just after eleven and skirted Main Street to avoid being caught again by Moran. He went to Tate's house, hammered on the front door, and waited impatiently for Nora to respond. A curtain at the window beside the door was twitched aside and Nora peered out at him. She shook her head emphatically and dropped the curtain. Grove could not believe what was happening and hammered on the door.

Once more Nora lifted the curtain and shook her head. She looked as if she had been crying. He pointed to the door but she shrugged and dropped the curtain. Grove's immediate reaction was to kick the door open, but he controlled his anger and departed. He had the stagecoach to meet, and afterwards he would see Tate at the bank and have a real set-to with the domineering banker.

★ ★ ★

Moran entered the saloon, gun in hand, and went to Brannigan's office. He shouldered the door open and strode inside. The office was empty. He went into the bar room, saw Sharkey, the bartender, doing his chores, and holstered the gun. There was no sign of Brannigan.

'Where's Brannigan?' Moran demanded.

Sharkey looked up. 'He went out a few minutes ago,' he replied. 'I don't know where he's gone or how long he'll be.'

'And where are Manning and Woodson?'

'I ain't seen them. If they were here they used the back door.'

Moran went to the batwings and studied the street from the doorway. He craned forward, pushing open the batwings, and looked towards the diner. There was no sign of the two hardcases. As he looked the opposite way along the street, wondering how

241

to handle the situation, a bullet splintered the batwing he was holding ajar and the crash of a pistol boomed from the direction of the diner.

Moran ducked back into the saloon, shaking his head. It had to be Manning, he thought, and pulled his gun. He cocked the weapon and thrust the batwings open. When he risked a glance along the street he saw Del Manning coming along the sidewalk. Gun smoke drifted around the small killer when he opened fire. Slugs tore into the woodwork around Moran. He lifted his Colt. The foresight was covering Manning's chest when he fired. The butt of the gun kicked against his hand as the weapon recoiled. Manning was diving sideways when the slug hit him. He fell on the sidewalk and then rolled off it into the street, raising dust.

A gun blasted from inside the saloon and Moran hurled himself to one side. His head jerked around and he saw the bartender in the act of taking fresh aim at him with a pistol he had lifted from

under the bar. Moran triggered a shot. Sharkey dropped his gun and dropped sideways out of sight. Gun smoke drifted across the saloon.

Moran got up and ran to the rear of the saloon. He went out to the back lots in double quick time and cocked his pistol as he sprinted along the alley beside the saloon to the main street. He paused in the alley mouth and peered out at the street, expecting to see Manning down in the dust. But there was no sign of the killer. A gun cut loose at him from back along the street in the direction of the diner, and he sought cover with slugs splintering woodwork around him.

He returned along the alley to the rear lot and went left to sprint towards the back of the diner. He found an alley beside the eating house and turned into it. A man was standing in the alley mouth at the street end, a gun in his hand, and he was wearing soldier's uniform. Moran recognized the tall figure of Tolliver. He went forward at a

run. Tolliver heard his footsteps and turned. He lifted his gun and advanced a couple of yards towards Moran, who triggered a shot. Tolliver fell on his face and remained motionless.

Moran paused beside Tolliver, saw that he was dead, and picked up the discarded gun. As he straightened, a figure appeared in the alley-mouth — another soldier; Levin.

'Throw up your hands,' Moran rasped. His gun clicked as he thumbed back the hammer.

Levin showed his teeth in a snarl and swung up his pistol. Moran's gun blasted and a scarlet blossom appeared on the front of Levin's tunic. The impact of the .45 slug threw Levin against the wall. He slid to the ground, his face scraping against the boards.

Moran stepped over the body and went out to the street. The diner was on his right; he flattened against the front wall and craned sideways to peer through the big front window. There were several diners seated at tables

inside, but Woodson and Manning were not present. Moran wondered about Manning as he looked around the street. He thought he had at least badly wounded the gunman. The acrid taste of gun smoke was sharp in his teeth.

There was no one in sight along the whole length of Main Street. Moran stepped back into the alley mouth. Where were Woodson and Manning? There was no sign of Brannigan. He thought about the bank, and realized that he should warn the banker about the proposed bank robbery. He went along the alley to the back lots and continued to the right until he reached the alley beside the bank.

Moran's ears were throbbing from the recent shooting. His head ached from the blow Manning had struck him. He kept moving, continuing past the rear of the bank until he reached the alley beside the law office. The back door was bolted and he went on to the street. A few townsmen were beginning to show themselves here and there

along Main Street. Moran went to the law-office door, and was not surprised when it opened to his touch. He entered. The front office was deserted and he went into the cell block.

The jailer, Colton, was standing in a locked cell, gripping the bars of the door. His face took on a grin of relief when he saw Moran, who hurried back into the office, found the cell keys lying in a corner, and released Colton.

'Say, I'm mighty pleased to see you,' the jailer said. 'You ain't gonna believe this, but Brannigan, the saloon man, came in here, pulled a gun on me and released those two soldiers you brought in last night, also that crooked gambler. I thought they were gonna kill me.'

'I took care of the deserters,' Moran said. 'Have you any idea where Brannigan and Gaines went? I didn't see them around the street, and I need to do something about them before they try to nail me.'

'They went off together, and I heard Brannigan saying something about

checking on Buller, over at the doc's place. I don't reckon he'll be there now, with all the shooting that's been going on. I wish the sheriff was back in town. He'd know how to handle this.'

'He won't be coming back.' Moran explained what he had heard in the saloon.

Colton dropped heavily into the seat behind the desk in the office, stunned by the news of Steadman's death. He opened his mouth to comment but closed it again and shook his head soundlessly. Then he sprang up and grasped Moran's arm.

'I heard the gambler tell Brannigan that Mrs Rogers had told you everything she knew about Buller and what was going on around town. Where did she go when you turned her loose? You'd better look her up. I've got a nasty feeling Gaines went after her when he got out of here.'

Moran turned instantly and hurried out of the office. He hastened along the street to the hotel, where Byron Slessor

was standing in front of the reception desk.

'Where's Mrs Rogers?' Moran demanded.

'I haven't seen her this morning,' Slessor replied. 'I thought you had her locked in the jail for safe keeping.'

'I turned her loose earlier this morning. Buller was going to kill her last night but he isn't in a fit condition to harm her, and I arrested the two deserters who left the fort with Buller yesterday. But the situation changed this morning. Brannigan went into the law office and busted the prisoners loose. The gambler, Gaines, said something about coming here to deal with Mrs Rogers.'

Moran was moving to the stairs as he spoke, and Slessor accompanied him. They ascended quickly, and Moran led the way to Mrs Rogers's room. He knocked at the door and waited for a reply. Interminable moments passed; he grew impatient and tried the door. It opened to his touch and he went into the room, his right hand on his

holstered gun butt. The room was empty. Moran turned quickly and departed. He feared that Gaines had taken Mrs Rogers, and there was only one place he could go.

Slessor followed Moran out of the hotel and along the sidewalk to the saloon. Moran hit the batwings with his left shoulder and lunged inside. A gun fired instantly inside the saloon and the bullet bored through the swing door. Moran hurled himself to the right in a low dive, looking for the source of the shot. He saw gun smoke drifting above the bar; Gaines was behind it with a pistol gripped in his hand. There was no sign of Mrs Rogers.

Moran triggered a shot at Gaines and the gambler ducked. Moran kept moving. He scrambled to his feet and hurled himself at the bar, leaping at the last instant to land on the polished top. He slid forward until he could cover the area behind the bar, and saw Gaines beginning to push himself up for another shot.

'Drop it!' Moran yelled.

Gaines looked up quickly. His face changed expression when he saw Moran covering him. He paused as if about to surrender, then hurled himself to the right and jerked his gun muzzle in Moran's direction. Moran fired. His slug smacked into the front of Gaines's coat. Gaines fell on his face and remained inert. Gun echoes faded slowly. Moran looked around and saw Slessor crouching by the end of the bar, his face exhibiting a blend of shock and fear.

'Take a look around the saloon,' Moran rasped. 'Mrs Rogers has got to be here somewhere.'

Slessor hurried across to Brannigan's office. Moran went to the stairs leading to the rooms overhead. He had mounted two stairs when Slessor's voice sounded.

'Mrs Rogers is here in the office, and she looks OK.'

Moran went down to the office and found Mrs Rogers roped to a chair.

Slessor was untying her.

'Are you OK?' Moran asked her. When she nodded he said, 'I'll talk to you later.'

Moran left the saloon and crossed the street to the doctor's house. Townsmen were moving along the sidewalks towards the law office. He entered the doctor's office. Doc Yelding was seated at his desk, roped to the chair, and a cloth was stuffed into his mouth. Buller was motionless on the examination couch. Moran saw fresh blood on Buller's chest.

Moran released the doctor. Yelding pulled the gag from his mouth.

'Brannigan came in,' he said in a gasping tone. 'He struck me with a pistol barrel and then hogtied me. I told him Buller was not well enough to be moved and he shot the sergeant dead when there was shooting along the street. It was cold-blooded murder. What's come over Brannigan? He must be loco, killing a man like that.'

'It looks like he's tying up loose

ends in his crooked business,' Moran observed. He glanced at a clock on the wall. The hands were pointing to ten minutes to noon. 'Stay under cover for a spell, Doc,' he advised. 'There's gonna be a bank robbery in a few minutes, and more shooting likely.'

Moran went to the street door, opened it a fraction and peered out. More men were on the sidewalks; one of them was Sergeant Grove, striding along the opposite sidewalk as if he was on parade at the fort, his blue uniform standing out among the drab clothing of the townsmen. Moran looked to the right. The bank was off in that direction, and two men were tying their horses to a hitch rail in front of the building. One of the animals was a grey, and Del Manning, his left shoulder bloodstained, stood beside it, checking his deadly pistol. The other man was Jake Woodson.

The street door of the bank opened and Brannigan appeared in the doorway. The saloon man's face was pale,

set in a mask of determination. He shouted at Woodson, who hurried into the bank, followed closely by Manning. The door closed abruptly. Moran drew his gun and checked its loads, thumbing fresh shells into its empty chambers. He looked around for Sergeant Grove but there was no sign of him. He shook his head, aware that he needed some gun help.

He left the doctor's house and crossed the street, heading for the alley beside the bank. He peered along its length and saw Sergeant Grove standing at the side door of the bank. The door was opened and Grove pushed forward, both hands raised as if he was being denied entrance. He disappeared inside the bank and Moran heard the door slam. There was a small side window a few yards into the alley. Moran went to it and peered into the building.

He saw Woodson and Manning standing just inside the entrance by the main street door. Brannigan was with

them, talking forcefully, waving his arms to emphasize his words. Grove and the banker were approaching the crooked trio, and Brannigan began to get excited. Manning moved to a seat by the entrance and dropped wearily into it. He drew his pistol and checked it, then pointed the weapon at Sergeant Grove and squeezed the trigger. Grove jumped as if he had been kicked by a mule. His hands lifted to his chest as he twisted and then fell to the floor. Brannigan froze, his face showing horror. His mouth gaped, and the expression on his face turned to fear when Manning got to his feet and waggled his pistol.

The banker stood dumbfounded, staring down at the inert Grove. Moran could tell by the patch of blood on the sergeant's chest that the bullet had killed him instantly. Moran was shocked by the cold-blooded killing, but he made an effort to break through the freezing numbness swirling through his brain. He hurried back to the

street; cocked his gun. He went the main door of the bank and opened it. The heads of all those inside swung in his direction as he entered.

Moran saw that Manning was the first to react. The killer lunged to his left and lifted his gun with practised ease. Moran's muzzle followed Manning's quick movement and he triggered two shots. He did not wait to see the result but moved to his right, swinging the pistol to cover Woodson, who was in the act of making a fast draw. Out of the corner of his eye Moran saw Manning double up under the hammer blows of the initial two shots, his gun falling out of his hand as if it had suddenly become too heavy to hold. Moran fired at Woodson, getting his shot in first. The slug struck Woodson's gun arm just above the elbow. The weapon flew out of his hand and thudded on the floor at Brannigan's feet.

Woodson reached around his waist to the left side of his gunbelt and pulled a

knife from a sheath there. His hand flashed up above his shoulder and started down in a throwing arc. Moran fired again; this time his muzzle was centred on Woodson's chest. The bullet took the horse-thief dead centre and he staggered forward a couple of steps on rapidly weakening legs before dropping to his knees. He fell sideways, his knife thudding on the floor.

Moran was half-deafened by the heavy reverberations of the shooting. He saw the banker pulling a small gun out of a coat pocket, but the hammer seemed to snag in the material and Tate had trouble clearing it.

'Drop it!' Moran called, his voice sounding strangely muffled in his own ears.

Tate ignored the warning, pulled his gun clear of the pocket, and cocked it. His hands shook as he used both of them to bring the gun to bear. Moran waited until the last possible moment; when he realized that the banker was intent on trading lead he fired a single

shot. Tate bent forward at the waist when the slug bored through his heart. His trigger finger jerked spasmodically and the gun exploded. The muzzle was pointing downward at an angle of forty-five degrees when it fired.

The bullet struck Brannigan in the centre of his back as he bent to snatch up Woodson's gun. Brannigan uttered a cry and spun around. He put his left hand on the floor to prevent himself from pitching forward on to his face. His left knee went down and he paused, twisting to look at Moran, his fleshy face contorted by shock and fear. He tried to lift Woodson's gun into the aim but Tate's bullet had finished him and his life ran out swiftly. He dropped the gun, then followed it down in a quivering heap. His left leg kicked convulsively several times. Then the interior of the bank became uncannily still and silence swooped back as the shock of man-made thunder diminished.

Moran drew a deep breath as he

straightened. He paused to listen to the dying echoes of the quick gun blasts. His back was to the street door when he heard it being pushed open. He whirled, gun lifting, then halted the movement when he saw a grim-faced uniformed sergeant entering with several troopers bunched behind him. The sergeant halted and saluted.

'Sergeant Kline reporting with a detail as ordered, Captain,' he said. 'What can we do to help?'

Moran heaved a sigh as he considered; then he realized that the shooting was over. His investigation was at an end. He thought of the ruthless men he had come up against, and a long sigh escaped him as he looked at the motionless bodies of the men he had slain. Perhaps he was the most ruthless of them all.

Other titles in the
Linford Western Library:

BLIZZARD JUSTICE

Randolph Vincent

After frostbite crippled the fingers of his gun hand, Isaac Morgan thought his days of chasing desperadoes were over. But when steel-hearted Deputy US Marshal Ambrose Bishop rides into town one winter evening, aiming to bait a trap for a brutal gang which has been terrorizing the border, Morgan's peace is shattered. For after the lawman's scheme misfires, and the miscreants snatch the town judge's beautiful daughter Kitty, Bishop and Morgan must join forces to get her back.

DYNAMITE EXPRESS

Gillian F. Taylor

Sheriff Alec Lawson has come a long way from the Scottish Highlands to Colorado. Life here is never slow as he deals with a kidnapped Chinese woman, moonshine that's turning its consumers blind, and a terrifying incident with an uncoupled locomotive which sees him clinging to the roof of a speeding train car. When a man is found dead out in the wild, Lawson wonders if the witness is telling him the whole truth, and decides to dig a little deeper . . .

HANGING DAY

Rob Hill

Facing the noose after being wrongfully convicted of his wife's murder, Josh Tillman breaks out of jail. Rather than go on the run, he heads home, determined to prove his innocence and track down the real killer. But he has no evidence or witnesses to back up his story; his father-in-law wants him dead; a corrupt prison guard is pursuing him; and the preacher who speaks out in his defence is held at gunpoint for his trouble . . .

APACHE SPRING

J. D. Kincaid

When a stagecoach bound for El Paso is held up by bandits, all but one of the passengers are massacred. Young Lizzie Reardon, a teacher about to take up a post in the school at Burro Creek, is the sole survivor — but, as she has seen the attackers' faces, she is now their target. Deputy Sheriff Frank McCoy joins forces with the famous Kentuckian gunfighter Jack Stone to defend her — but will they succeed?

LYNCHING AT PROSPECT FALLS

Jack Matthews

Town marshal Matt Walker becomes increasingly worried when his young nephew Joey Crane disappears on his way to visit his uncle. All clues point in the direction of Prospect Falls, a town owned and controlled by wealthy rancher H. J. Copeland of the Bar C — whose cattle are rustled on a regular basis. But the thieving gang is actually led by his own foreman, and anyone caught straying onto ranch land is lynched to divert attention from the real culprits . . .